Me
Three

By Susan Juby

PUFFIN CANADA

an imprint of Penguin Random House Canada Young Readers,
a division of Penguin Random House of Canada Limited

Published in hardcover by Puffin Canada, 2022

1 2 3 4 5 6 7 8 9 10

Jacket design by Lisa Jager
Jacket illustrations by Hartley Lin

Manufactured in Canada

Library and Archives Canada Cataloguing in Publication

Title: Me 3 / Susan Juby.
Other titles: Me three
Names: Juby, Susan, 1969- author.
Identifiers: Canadiana (print) 20210091312 | Canadiana (ebook)
20210091347 | ISBN 9780735268722 (hardcover) |
ISBN 9780735268739 (EPUB)
Classification: LCC PS8569.U324 M4 2022 | DDC jC813/.6—dc23

Library of Congress Control Number: 2020951913

www.penguinrandomhouse.ca

Penguin
Random House
PUFFIN CANADA

For Emily.

10 Rules for Living a Lucky Life

From the author of *Get Lucky: A Player's Guide to Poker* and the star of *Get Lucky TV!*

1. Don't take things personally.

2. Look for the upside.

3. Never show an unlucky hand.

4. Learn about people. Then learn about cards.

5. Put together a winning team.

6. You've got to answer the door when luck knocks.

7. Don't chase a losing streak.

8. If your cards keep coming up bad, change the deck.

9. Surf the waves of fortune.

10. Avoid the negative.

1

Hey, Larry,

I know you're really busy right now and will get back to me when you can. That's what your housekeeper said when I called your house because you didn't answer my texts or DMs. No problem, man. I get it, even though it's kind of weird not to talk to you for so long. I'm not taking any of it personally. That's the first Rule for Living a Lucky Life: Don't Take Things Personally!

But I thought I might write to you about how it's going here, so I don't forget anything when we finally talk again. Don't worry—I won't actually send you a whole bunch of letters. That would be weird. But I might use them for notes when my mom and my sister and I move back to Vegas and everything goes back to normal.

Hey! Do you think letters like this would work for our Personal Writing assignments? I know we're not allowed to take that course until seventh grade, but maybe this will help me get a head start.

3

The main thing I wanted to tell you is that it's impossible to let people know you used to be cool, especially when you can't tell them who you are. You can't just walk up to them and say: Hello there! You may not know this, but at my old school, I had friends and some people thought I was funny. A couple of girls, such as Trelawny Johnson, even said I was handsome or whatever. Explaining former social success is not cool. It's like a catch-23, or whatever that's called.

As you know better than anyone, Lar, the coolest thing about me was always my dad, and my mom says we can't mention him here. What good is having a dad who is a famous professional poker player who wrote *Get Lucky*, one of the best-selling poker books of all time, and who is also the star of *Get Lucky TV* if you can't mention it? You know how it is since your mom is the head producer of *Get Lucky TV*, and we get to share in the glory together. Anyway, the point is that we're using my mom's last name until "things settle down." Whatever that means.

Which reminds me, I'm sorry about your mom and everyone else who lost their jobs when the show got canceled. My dad says it's just temporary until everything gets figured out. As soon as that happens, everyone can go back to work, and we can come home, and things will get back to how they used to be. I just want you to know none of what they're saying is true. Missy Stephenson is not telling the truth. My dad didn't do what she said. He would never do that to someone, especially not a celebrity guest who is also a movie star. I really hope you know that. My dad's whole job is taking famous people to high-stakes games. As if he would ever do something to one of them!

You might be wondering why we just disappeared a couple of weeks ago. Maybe you're even a little mad about it. Well, we had this family meeting, and my dad explained the misunderstanding that happened at work. It was pretty bad. The meeting, I mean. No one likes family meetings, unless they're about where to go on holiday. Even then they're not that fun in our family because my sister hates sunshine and joy. But this meeting was extra bad.

My mom didn't speak the whole time. My dad said he had to go away for a while because of the misunderstandings and false accusations. But he promised it would all work out and that we should follow his Rule #2 for Having a Lucky Life: Look for the Upside. As you know, my dad's English accent always makes him sound like he knows what he's talking about and like you can trust him.

My mom and Kate were so upset we didn't really finish our terrible family meeting, which was a relief. But right after, like the same day, my mom made me and Kate pack up our stuff and she drove us here, and my dad went to a treatment center for people who are having problems, like being addicted to drugs or gambling, which is quite sardonic (I think that's the word?) seeing as he's a professional poker player and gambling is sort of his job, or it used to be. I guess in his case he's staying there to help with how it feels to be misunderstood for being funny and friendly and maybe giving a few too many hugs to celebrities who aren't used to being touched so they accuse you of taking liberties and ruin your whole life, and the lives of your children.

You might not even know where we are since you aren't reading my messages. My mom and sister and I moved to my mom's cousin's house in Stony Butte, Arizona, to get away from everything for a while. We have been here for two weeks now, and today is the first day of sixth grade. Even though our school in Vegas, Circle Square, has its issues, such as too much talking about what color our feelings are, it's about a thousand times better than Stony Butte Elementary, at least so far. I'm writing this on my lunch break, so maybe things will get better? I wore my Doug Stokes shirt. Remember when we got those? Anyway, I thought people might notice it, but so far nothing. Probably should have worn my Van Johnson shirt. I was going to save that T-shirt for tomorrow.

Okay, well, you'll probably never read this, but even so, I hope your first day was good. I don't want to say I miss you and Trelawny and Emily and Monty, the whole first-name-ends-with-a-*y* Circle Square gang, because that would be embarrassing, but I do sort of wish I was there.

Keep it casual!

Rodney

2

Hey, Larry,

Okay, so I have to tell you about the afternoon.

If the first morning at Stony Butte was lame, the first afternoon was . . . whatever is a lot worse than lame.

Here's the deal. I know you'll appreciate this. Like I said before, I wore my Doug Stokes T-shirt. Remember how when we showed up at Circle Square last year with our Doug Stokes shirts, everyone was impressed, and they wanted to hear about how he came to my house for a pool party and a barbecue, and you and your mom were there, and we got some major points for that? So I was happy when the kid who sat next to me in homeroom noticed my shirt after lunch.

"Who's that?" he asked, after staring at the big picture of Doug's face.

"Doug Stokes," I said. I thought he would say awesome or ask where I got it. I was ready to tell him how Doug was a nice guy, even though my dad said that for a smart guy, he's terrible at poker, and how my friend Larry and I went to a taping of his show. I hoped that would give me a chance to get the conversation going so I could implement Rule #4 for Living a Lucky Life: Learn about People. I was relying on my Doug shirt to get things rolling.

"Who's Doug Smokes?" asked the kid. He is massive and has dark hair in a flattop brush cut. He looks like he might ride BMX or motocross or something. He looks like the kind of kid who might have a gun that his dad gave him.

"Stokes," I said. "Not Smokes. You don't know him? He's the star of *The Doug Stokes Show*. It's super funny. He makes fun of people who don't believe in science or climate change or evolution and people who think the earth is flat and religious people who don't understand about dinosaurs. He's hilarious."

The kid narrowed his eyes, which probably wasn't easy because they already were practically closed from how angry and suspicious he was.

"What did you say?" he said, his voice low.

"I'm sorry?" I knew I'd messed up somewhere, but I wasn't sure where. You're better than me at reading people. Maybe you would have known to be quiet. Unfortunately, I didn't.

"Did you say religious people are dumb?"

I felt myself start to blink, which I do when I get stressed. I never used to blink much. That has changed since we moved to Stony Butte. These days I'm a blink lord.

"No," I said, sounding weaselly, even to myself. "I never said that. I'm quoting Doug."

"God is no joke, and He will strike down anyone who sullies his name," said the kid.

"Oh." I'd heard of people like this kid, but I never met one before.

"I should punch you in the face," he said. "For making fun of God."

"I'm sorry. I, uh, didn't mean to. I like God." I said this even though I don't know anything about God because my parents messed up big time and forgot to teach me any religion. "Doug is just—that's his shtick, I guess. Making fun of people who don't, uh, agree with him."

"What's a shtick?" asked the kid. I didn't say anything because what if I made him even madder? I didn't answer, but he kept going, getting more worked up. You would have freaked out if you were there, Larry. Seriously. It was bad.

"Shut up," he said, even though I didn't say anything. "Before I shut you up."

The kids around us were staring, and not in an I-feel-your-pain kind of way. Except for a girl sitting at the table next to us, who looked curious. She had a single braid wrapped around her head about four times.

"Did you meet him?" she asked. "Doug Stokes?"

Relief! Someone understood that it was cool to know Doug Stokes!

"Yeah. He came over for a party at our house. Our old house, I mean. Where we lived before here. We had a bar-becue and everyone swam in the pool, including Doug. He came over to play p—I mean, there were a lot of people there. It was awesome. If you knew Doug like I knew Doug—" I said.

"A pool?" interrupted the girl. "An aboveground? Or an inflatable?"

"Uh, no. It was a proper pool. Olympic size."

She made a sound like she was spitting out a bug and then repeated my words in a high-pitched voice. "He came over for a party and swam in our *proper* in-the-ground *pool. Olympic-sized.*"

"Oooooh," said a guy sitting behind me. "I had no idea my grandma's aboveground pool wasn't proper."

A bunch of other kids were snickering. It was time to shut up. I stared down at my desk. I wanted to get up and move away from the angry God-defending boy and the angry in-ground-pool-hater girl, but I was too scared. I wanted to button my long-sleeved shirt up over Doug's face. You know how the only sports we've ever really done are Ping-Pong and a little bit of water polo? Well, my advice to you is to take up boxing and maybe running. Because Ping-Pong and water polo leave a person defense-less against attack. I never thought I'd need self-defense. You don't need it when you have friends.

At least no one punched me on the first day, so that's something. I kept my mouth shut for the rest of school so I wouldn't make anyone else mad. I also kept my shirt buttoned up so no one would see Doug's face. Just like me, Doug wasn't popular here.

Like I said before, I hope your first day of sixth grade was better than mine was. We've been here for two weeks and it feels like six years.

TTYS. Or not.

Rodney

3

Hey, Larry,

Me again. I thought you might like to know more about where we are and about my second day at the lamest school in the world. The house is kind of interesting and also depressing. It's small and old and not too nice, but the walls are covered in these big photos that my mom's cousin Maria took. They're pictures of her mountaineering and rock climbing, so they show incredible skies and mountaintops and cliffs and people sleeping in slings on the sides of mountains. Maria's pictures make me feel like I should go outside more. Maybe we should go to a climbing wall when I get back. You'd probably be good at climbing. Remember that time we went to that basketball player's house in Los Angeles for my dad's show? It was me and you and my dad and your mom and the crew, and the player had an actual full-sized climbing wall in his house. And a full-sized basketball court. And a home theater with those big fancy chairs. Remember how we didn't do any

11

sports, even though the player said we could? Instead, we went to his theater room and watched *Black Panther* for, like, the fourth time and ate proper movie popcorn until your mom made us go back to the hotel? That was a fun one.

Anyway, so the photos are nice. But that's about it. Everything else in the house is old, like it-came-from-a-dumpster old, because Maria doesn't believe in buying new things. She sure wouldn't like life in Vegas much!

Stony Butte Elementary is sort of like Maria's house, minus the cool photos. It's about three hundred years old and smells like someone ate a couple of pounds of glue and then barfed it back up.

Maria's house is right on the edge of town, near one of the buttes, which are big rocks that stick up in the air. They remind me of Tonka toys a giant forgot to pick up. The butte closest to us has two rounded parts on top and it looks like a big bum in the sky. Seriously. It's kind of crazy. The rock butts are the only reason this town exists, far as I can tell. People come here to climb them and mountain bike up them and jump off them. Quite a few Western movies have been filmed here, as my mom has pointed out about twelve hundred times, because she seems to think that will make me like Stony Butte more. Does anyone under sixty even watch Western movies?

Here's an interesting thing. Yesterday, my mom picked us up after school, but from now on I have to walk home alone. Can you imagine us doing that at Circle Square? The teachers would have called the authorities! Mom says we have to walk home alone every day because she is going to be busy working and because she can't afford to have someone come and pick us up. It's no fun being broke, but when my dad gets out of treatment, he can play a few big games and he'll be back on top and things can go back to normal. Rule #6 for Living a Lucky Life: You've Got to Answer the Door When Luck Knocks. At least I think that's the rule that fits best here.

I guess Maria, who travels all over the world with her girlfriend who's also a climber, said we could stay as long as we want if we pay her mortgage. Considering how not-nice her house is, it's probably about five dollars a month.

Anyway, today I was about halfway home from school when someone rode up beside me on a BMX bike. No helmet! Who rides a bike without head protection?

He nodded his helmet-less head at me and I nodded back.

"I'm in your class," he said, pedaling slowly. I'd never seen anyone pedal that slowly before. You'd have been impressed.

"Oh," I said.

"I'm Ben," he said.

I was so shocked by the no-helmet thing that I didn't know what to say.

Then Ben jumped his bike on and off the curb sideways and sort of swung it around 180 degrees under him. With no helmet!

"Don't worry about Chum," said Ben when he was beside me again. "He goes to my church, but he hasn't quite figured out the whole peaceful thing. He probably won't punch you. He likes to threaten people he knows he can beat up. If he punches you, he's not doing it for God. He's doing it because he can't control his emotions."

Then Ben turned his bike around and started riding backwards! He was the best bike rider I've ever seen. He turned around so he was going forward again and stopped his bike and moved it back and forth in place. It was like magic.

When I got over the shock of how good a rider Ben was, I noticed that he talked like a Circle Square kid. I wasn't expecting that from a kid from Stony Butte. I also wondered about Chum's name. My dad calls people chum sometimes. It's British for "friend," but it's also a kind of fish that you feed to other fish. Either way, it's a strange name.

"Our pastor's working with Chum, but he's kind of a case. Probably has home trouble. Same with Lallie. She's the girl with the braid. She gets offended a lot. It's kind of her thing. I wouldn't take it personally. Does your house here have a pool?" he asked.

It was interesting that he said the thing about not taking things personally. Maybe Ben read my dad's book! Obviously, I couldn't ask him, but I wondered.

I shook my head.

"Bummer," said the kid. "I'd like to know someone with a pool. Guess I'll have to keep looking. Nice to meet you. Okay, I gotta go."

"Bye," I said, and he waved back at me as he rode away.

Somehow, just from that one little talk I felt better about the day, which wasn't quite as bad as the first one. It made me think I could survive living in Stony Butte until we could go home.

At the end of the block, I could see our little house, all by itself. It has exactly no trees around it and the street and the sidewalk ends right in front of it. Kaput. No more street. Past the house are dirt trails that head off into the park toward the butte, but they are only for bikes and hikers. Last stop before the butt. That's us.

I let myself in with the key. The house was dark, but I could hear noise coming from Kate's room. My mom was at an appointment with an employment counselor.

Here's the thing: I might be able to handle living in Stony Butte for a while, but I wonder if Kate can. I really think I might be better at coping with change than she is. I know you think Kate is awesome because she's actually nice to you, but you don't have to live with her. You're lucky not to have a sister.

She's been losing weight ever since we got here. And she had no weight to lose because she's been on a diet since she was ten. I paid enough attention in our health class to know that's not healthy. I still remember when your mom tried to talk to Kate about how eating properly is a human right and how she should claim her space in the world by staying strong and healthy. Only your mom could talk to Kate like that. Kate'd take my head off if I tried. Right now, she's not eating carbs, and my mom says she's worried about her, but she can't really say anything about it because she's not eating carbs either.

To be honest, I'm not even sure what carbs are. All I know is that they're in most things that are delicious, such as chips, fries, candy, and pop. Also, beets and cashews. I know this because my mom and my sister had a huge fight last night because my mom made a dish that had beets and cashew butter in it, and my sister said she wouldn't eat it because of carbs, and my mom said Kate was taking things too far, and Kate said maybe my mom didn't take things far enough.

I have no idea what she meant and I don't want to know.

I don't get involved in the negativity or arguments. After all, Rule #10 literally says: Avoid the Negative. I also try to mind my own business, which is why I didn't want to tell Kate I was home. But it's also important to be friendly, so I knocked anyway. I tried to do it in a casual way, not a checking up on her way. The not-eating thing makes me want to check on her a lot. She hates that. I guess because it's negative. I don't know. You were always better than me at following that rule.

"What?" she said through her door, which is all scuffed up like all the doors in the house.

"I'm home."

"Duh," she said. Kate doesn't think it's important to be friendly or easygoing. I think it's from not enough carbs, probably. Not that I'd ever risk my life by saying that to her.

"Have a good day?" I asked.

"Oh my god," she said. "Enough already, Rodney."

"Okay," I said. She still hates it when I'm nice. She says I do it on purpose to make her look bad. She only has two friends, and I think it's because she's not relaxed or easygoing or nice. Not that I can judge right now. I currently seem to have no friends. Oops. Sorry. That sounded bad. I know we're still friends. Or we will be when we start talking again.

I went into the living room and sat on the couch. I didn't feel like going in my room because then I would have to think about how small my new room is. It's basically like what most people would use for a closet. It might actually have even been a closet, for all I know. My mom has a proper bedroom and my sister has a proper bedroom and I got an eighth of a room. It feels like a coffin, sort of. None of us even has an en suite bathroom. My sister would probably have started a human rights complaint if my mom made her take the closet-coffin, and I don't mind, really. I just don't like spending time in there. Sometimes, though, I wish Missy Stephenson could see my new coffin room so she could see what lying does to other people. Maybe then she'd tell the truth and we wouldn't have to hide out in Stony Butte anymore.

I was about to start up *Death Spawn 4*, but then Kate stomped into the living room.

"Don't start blasting that stupid game," she said. I know you think Kate is pretty, but she's really not. She's especially not pretty here. Girls here all dress like they're going camping. Kate dresses like she wants to hurt people's eyes. She's cutting her hair even worse than usual and wearing even uglier old-man sweaters and old-man pants, and she's barely even cleaning the lenses of her huge glasses, so I have no idea how she can see. Maybe she can't. Maybe that's the point.

She fit in at the Vegas Academy, but not here. I doubt people here get her at all. They're probably even less into Kate's fashion sense than they are into my Doug T-shirt.

I was going to tell her I could wear my headphones, but she had a mean look on her face, so I went to watch the new Van Johnson video. Remember the episode where my dad played poker with Van and his Johnson Boys? I wish we could have gone to that one. Oh well, at least we got T-shirts. Which reminds me that I didn't wear my Van Johnson T-shirt today because people here don't seem to understand T-shirts. But Kate wasn't done with me.

"I need you to help me with something later," she said.

"What?"

"A blood test."

"A what?"

"A blood test."

"You should go to a doctor for that," I told her.

"Not that kind of blood test," she said. "A ketosis meter. I have to check my levels."

I thought it might have something to do with carbs and that made me nervous. I'm getting super nervous about carbs in general. You're lucky your mom is not bizarre about food.

"Get Mom to help you."

"She doesn't know I bought the meter. I used her credit card."

I didn't want to do it, but I also didn't want to say no. My sister was scary even before we moved here. Now she's a Death Star of bad mood.

Instead of answering, I put my headphones on and watched the video. I really wish you were here to help Kate. I'm not good with blood.

Take care.

Rodney

4

Hey, Larry,

Hope this finds you well. I'm okay, except for a few things. Like, I wonder how everybody is. Did Monty get an accent when he went with his parents to France? Remember how he got one when they went to Australia for a month and it lasted for almost the whole term?

Things here are fine although not at dinner. My dad always calls when we're having dinner.

He calls my phone because my mom and my sister won't pick up when they see his number, which is mean of them, but I don't say that because it would get them started. Tonight, I answered. Like I always do.

"Hey, Rodney," he said.

"Hi, Dad."

"You guys having dinner?"

"Yeah."

"What's on the menu this evening?"

You will be disgusted to know that my mom and my sister were having salad with tofu and nuts, but only the kind of nuts that have almost no carbs. I was having a previously frozen chicken pot pie because salad doesn't fill me up.

"Salad and stuff," I said.

"Sorry to hear it," he said. That made me smile. My dad gets things.

"And school?" He'd been asking that question every day since we got here, even though school just started three days ago. He even asks on weekends. My dad isn't that good at keeping track of time. At least this time I could give him a new answer.

"Pretty good."

"Bet those kids don't know what hit them. Couple of bright, dashing sorts like you and Kate come along to shake things up."

"Yeah," I said, because that was how it should have gone and, also, my dad had enough on his mind without me telling him how people were not at all excited to meet me.

"Your mother around?" He knew she was. My mom always eats with us so she can try to make Kate eat all the nuts on her salad. "Might I have a word?"

My chest got tight, but I held out the phone to my mom, who was sitting across from me. Her face got tight, which was strange to see, because before we moved here my mom always had a really soft, nice face. Still, she took the phone, got up from the table, and went into her room.

"He is such a jerk," said Kate.

"He is not," I said.

She started talking, but I ignored her and dug my fork into the pot pie. You would love these pies. I found them at the local grocery store in the frozen section. My mom was buying stuff for smoothies and sent me to get frozen raspberries. I came back with four pot pies. The label says they are made by a local lady who calls herself Mrs. Perfect Pie. She's got good self-esteem and she's right about her pies. They are super tall. Like pot-pie volcanoes. So far they are the best thing about living here. Not to be negative. I put my fork into the pastry on top and a cloud of steam puffed out, which was satisfying.

"Ugh, that thing is full of trans fats," said Kate, who does not like to see people enjoying themselves. That's what my dad used to say when she criticized our food at dinner. My dad isn't very skinny, and he says it's because he enjoys his food too much. He says Kate needs to start eating normally because she's too skinny. But he also used to tease my mom if she ate too much, even though my mom is very skinny from doing so much Pilates and yoga and stuff.

My mom's voice was rising in the bedroom. They were arguing now. I ignored it and lifted the whole pastry top like a lid. You can't enjoy a pot pie properly if you've got a burned tongue.

"How about next time you *don't* answer the phone when Dad calls?" said Kate. "Maybe then we can have one lousy meal without a big argument and Mom in tears and the whole dysfunctional dinner package?"

I rolled up the pastry top into the world's tastiest transfat burrito and ate it. If I ever meet Mrs. Perfect, I plan to shake her hand and tell her she's a genius. I'll definitely bring a few Mrs. Perfects when we come home.

"Thank you for asking how my third day was," said Kate. "It was amazing. I joined band, was invited over for a sleepover by three intellectually fascinating girls, and a number of handsome and sensitive boys asked me on dates."

I stared at her.

"Gotcha," she said. "My day was terrible, thanks. People here are incredibly lame. And you? How was your day?"

I shrugged and went back to digging the peas out of my pot pie. I like to take them out and eat them on their own so I can really enjoy them. The pea is an underestimated legume. As soon as I had that thought, I thought of how you're always talking about underestimated things. I, for one, appreciate it. I also appreciate how we both have excellent vocabularies for our age and both want to be writers. Nobody else here seems to care about stuff like that.

After that, I saw that Kate was taking all of the pumpkin seeds and sunflower seeds out of her salad and forking them into her napkin.

"Too many carbs," she whispered. We heard my mom's door open, and my sister folded up the napkin and stuck it inside her giant man-pants' pocket.

Mom stood at the counter and wiped her eyes. The cry-calls make dinner extra unfun. I had twelve peas out of the pie and my eye on at least five more. I was looking forward to getting as many of them as possible on my fork. Peas are probably super high in carbs.

"We're going to see your father this weekend," said my mom in a croaky voice.

My sister's head jerked up, but I kept looking for peas in my pie. We haven't seen my dad since we moved here, and even though I miss him, I sort of don't want to see him. Do you ever feel like that about your dad? I mean, since he and your mom got divorced?

"I disrespectfully decline the invitation," said Kate.

"That is not an option. I am not leaving you here alone."

"There are only about seventeen people in this town," said Kate. "And I'm scarier than any of them."

"We'll leave very early in the morning on Saturday so we can be home in the afternoon. I have a job interview."

"On a Saturday?" said my sister. "What kind of salt mines job are you applying for anyway?"

When my sister gets like this, she will fight with anyone about anything.

"It's a job in insurance. That's the day that's best for the manager."

Kate made a disgusted noise.

"Well, then we better not go see Jeremy at the spa. Don't want you to miss your interview."

My sister has started calling my dad by his first name to show her disrespect. She says he's at a "spa" even though she knows he's at a treatment center to help him cope with the unfair situation.

I had almost eight amazing peas on my fork when my sister turned on me.

"Rodney, isn't it time we talked more about why we're going to see Jeremy at his *spa* instead of living with him. In. Our. House?"

23

"Kate, leave him alone. Let him process this in his own time," said my mom.

"So he gets to live in his little bubble, all happy and oblivious, repeating Jeremy's dumb rules for luck, while the rest of us have to deal with reality?"

"He's not in a bubble," said my mom. "In fact, I think he's right on track. He's adjusting in his own way and at his own pace."

"I can't stand it," said my sister.

"We've discussed this, Kate," said my mom. "Each of us is allowed to deal with this in our own way."

Here's the thing: Kate keeps shoving her phone in my face to show me articles about my dad and what happened with Missy Stephenson and some other women who overreact to people being in their personal space. I never read them and try not to see the headlines. You can't trust what the media says, and I think my dad was right when he said those women were blowing everything out of proportion. I don't want a whole bunch of negative stuff stuck in my head. That makes it easier to follow Rule #3: Never Show an Unlucky Hand, which is what you're doing if you get all upset about stuff. If we all keep looking for the upside (Rule #2), we'll be back in Vegas, and Mom can get back to her barre and Pilates classes and having lunch with her friends, and my sister can get back to her art school and hanging out with her angry and depressed friends, and I can get back to having a good life and to you guys.

That reminds me, who is your partner for the science fair? I bet you picked Monty. Good choice. But you guys

24

will still get beaten by Emily and Trelawny. They have no sense of perspective about competition.

But back to the dinner situation. I got all the peas except one on my fork, which isn't easy. I am pretty good. It's like we understand each other, me and peas.

I ate them and they were delicious.

"Can I be excused?" I said.

"Of course, honey," said my mother. I looked at her then and she smiled. My mom has the best smile, even when she's tired.

I hope she gets to start smiling again soon.

Anyway, I probably won't see you on Saturday. Mom says we're just going to the treatment center and then home. But maybe I'll send you a text or something.

Rodney

PS: I did help my sister with her blood sample. I had to hand her a ketosis strip after she stabbed her finger with this little jabber to get a drop of blood. She said I had to be there in case she fainted. I nearly fainted myself when she squeezed the blood onto the strip and then stuck it in a little machine. But she was happy because the machine gave her a good number. I don't know what ketosis is or why she wants to have it in her blood, but I bet it's not healthy and that my mom would be so upset if she found out. Thought you might appreciate how weird our family is.

5

Hey, Larry,

Today our math teacher, Miss Jenkins, gave us a pop quiz to assess our skill level. Miss Jenkins is smiley but she's also sort of mean. Evidence: quiz on day four.

I could tell the kid in the next desk was lost, so I helped him out just like you used to do for me. I nodded at my paper in front of me and he understood right away.

After I showed him the answer, he nodded in my general direction. He was normal looking, unlike lots of the other kids in my class who seem too strong or too tall or like they don't have showers to get clean but instead jump in rivers and then roll around on rocks like otters. I think it might be from all the outdoor activities people around here do. The kids look old, and the adults dress like kids. It's strange.

After class, the kid I helped leaned over to me. "Thanks. Who gives a test in the first week?"

"Yeah," I said. I didn't mention that in my old school we'd learned about multiplying and dividing decimals a long time ago and that the quiz the teacher gave us was totally easy.

"I'm Dave," he said. "You going for lunch?" He is a white kid with short brown hair and round glasses.

I'd been planning to sit near my locker by myself and play games or maybe write to you, but that wasn't going to get me any more friends. A person needs to have online friends and real ones for a healthy mix. I currently have none anywhere, which isn't great.

I semi-shrugged, because I didn't know if he was asking if I wanted to join him and his friends or just asking a general question. For about the hundred and fiftieth time, I wished I was back at Circle Square with you guys.

"I'm going to eat out by the benches. You can come if you want," said Dave.

"Sure," I said, because Rule #4 is Learn about People and Rule #5 is Put Together a Winning Team. You can't do either of those things when you don't talk to anyone.

We got our lunches, and I followed him down the hall.

He had to go to the bathroom but he told me where to meet him outside.

There were two girls sitting on the benches. They looked at me when I stopped near them.

I recognized them from my class and they looked as normal as Dave, which was a relief.

One of the girls whispered something to the other.

"Don't whisper, Macii," said the girl with nearly white hair and dark-blue eyes and brown eyebrows.

28

Macii looked embarrassed. "I said that's the guy," she said. Then she looked at me. "Sorry."

What did she mean? Was she talking about me because I was new? Or because of my first-day Doug shirt and our pool?

"Macii likes to talk in whispers," said her friend. "She says it's a shyness thing."

Macii nodded. "It is," she whispered.

"It's also a gossipy thing," said her friend.

"Hey!" said Dave, as he came through the door.

I was relieved to see him.

"Everyone, this is . . . What's your name again?" he asked.

"Rodney," I said, and I didn't explain that I was named after this old comedian named Rodney Dangerfield who my dad loved. Trying to explain it would probably make me sound like a try-hard.

"Rodney just saved me in math," said Dave.

"Rigmor," said the white-haired girl.

"Rodney," I said.

Things were looking up, and not just because Dave was nice and Rigmor was pretty. These kids might have been from Circle Square. They had a sense of humor and enjoyed a little witty reportee, if that's the right word. You know—when people talk to each other in an amusing way. You'd probably like them. I started to think things would be okay at Stony Butte Elementary, at least for a little while.

"I've never heard that name before," I said.

"It's Norwegian," said Rigmor.

"Do you guys want to—" Before Rigmor could finish, the door to the school opened behind me and we all turned. When they saw who it was, their faces changed.

Chum stood in the doorway.

I could see from his angry red face that his emotional problems hadn't improved.

"Get out of here," he said, and all my new friends got up and left.

Wait! I wanted to say to Dave and Macii and Rigmor. *You forgot me!* Here's the thing, Lar. Even though you aren't speaking to me and didn't return the text I sent you a couple of days ago, I know you would never have left me alone if I was attacked by a giant with emotional problems. But I guess these people weren't going to get in the way of Chum kicking the snot out of me.

"You and me got some unfinished business," he said. I couldn't figure out why he was mad again now. He hadn't said anything to me for the past few days. He just glared at me when he caught my eye.

"Sorry about the shirt. I don't even think Doug Stokes is that funny anymore," I said. "He says a lot of dumb stuff. I'm probably even going to throw it out."

Chum's jaw was sticking out so I could see his lower teeth. He looked like one of those dogs who can hardly breathe. So I sort of laughed. Because nothing felt quite real. A few weeks ago, I had an awesome life. I was heading back to Circle Square with all my friends who had first names that ended in a *y*. You and I were going to try to come in second at the science fair and third in the school Ping-Pong tournament, and everything was great.

And now I was being menaced by a boy named Chum who had teeth like a dog. That reminds me, I actually looked it up and it turns out that the word "chum" has more than one meaning. It means friend, which he obviously is not, but it also means a kind of fish you use to feed to other fish or even sharks: it's not good to be chum or to be near one!

"I hate people like you," he said. "You helped Dave with that test just now but not me. Maybe you think you're better than me because . . ."

He couldn't think of why I was better. But I could. For the first time in my life, I was mean to someone on purpose.

"Because I'm smarter and less of a jerk?" I said. "Because I don't pick on people? Because my breath doesn't smell like pepperoni and boiled egg farts?"

You'd have freaked out, Lar. I was kind of aggro for the first time in my life.

His face got redder and he was starting to snort with rage, like a bull or my mom doing Breath of Fire during yoga.

That's when I remembered that I didn't know any self-defense and should keep my mouth shut, even if I was feeling sick of everyone and everything.

Things were getting out of hand. It was time to calm things down. Time to use my Circle Square training in conflict resolution: Defuse. De-escalate. Use your words!

"Look, Chum," I said in the calm voice our nanny used to use when we were driving her crazy.

"What did you call me?" He wasn't growling anymore. He was kind of screeching.

31

"Uh," I started. Before I could finish, he ran at me.

"DON'T CALL ME CHUM!" he screamed, and he picked me up. Like, all of me. He picked me up like a battering ram that he was going to use to bust down the first castle door he saw.

He ran out onto the playing field, carrying me under his giant arm. I was too shocked to do anything.

He was going full speed, and I could see other kids' shocked faces as we ran past, so he could smash my head into who knows what.

I think I went out-of-body for a minute or so. Like PTSD.

Chum is fast and huge, and I could see that we were heading for the soccer net at the end of the playing field. He was still giving this kind of warrior cry, and I didn't know whether to brace myself or go limp before we hit. A person could get a broken neck from being used as a battering ram, and I don't have such a strong neck to begin with.

"AAAAAGGHHHHHHH!" he said.

For some reason, I started yelling too.

"AAAAAAAGGGGHHHHH!" I said.

The two of us were yelling as loud as we could, and we were almost at the soccer net when I saw a blur out of the corner of my eye.

"AAAAAAAAGGGGHHHHHH!!" said the blur.

"AAAAGGGHHHHH?" said Chum.

"AAAAAAAGGGGHHHH?!" I said.

The blur got between Chum and me and the net and somehow headed us off. Chum lost his footing and we went down. He landed on me and it was like getting squashed by a stegosaurus. Knocked the wind right out of me.

"Ooof!" I said.

"Ugh," said Chum.

Once Chum climbed off me and my eyes uncrossed and my ears stopped ringing, I saw a boy standing there, holding his hands up like he was trying to calm things down.

"Fisherman," he said. "I thought we talked about this. You can't go smashing people into the soccer net every time you lose your temper."

"Yeah, but it's better than smashing them into a wall, right?" said Chum/Fisherman.

"I admit, the net is better. But it's still not great."

"He really made me mad," said Fisherman. He sounded calm, like he was talking about why he liked blueberry instead of raspberry Pop-Tarts.

The boy nodded. "But you made him yell with terror, so you're probably even." I realized then that it was Ben, the boy with the bike. He hadn't been back at school since the first day.

Fisherman nodded and started to smile. His face was no longer bright red. It was more rosy, I guess. He looked kind of funny when he smiled, as in humorous, not strange.

Then he laughed. His laugh was extremely high-pitched, and it was one of those laughs that makes everyone else want to laugh too.

I laughed in return and so did Ben.

"AAAAGGHHH!" said Fisherman.

"AAAAGGGHHH!" said Ben.

"AAAGG—" I stopped when Fisherman stopped laughing and looked at me. "Sorry," I said.

"Just kidding," said Fisherman. "You can laugh too."

And the three of us cracked up harder than I have since I left home. I have no idea why.

Anyway, I hope things are good with you. Can you believe the first week of sixth grade is almost over? I can't.

Take care,

Rodney

6

Hey, Larry,

So the big news is that we finally saw my dad. We left at six in the morning. I didn't mind the long drive, because we still have our Range Rover. My mom says it's worth as much as my cousin's house and that she should sell it because it's not practical, but I bet she's probably not going to sell it, since it's one of the only things we have left from our old life. Not as cool as when my dad had the Bentley. Remember when he used to drive us up and down the Strip in that? And how sometimes we got to throw packs of Get Lucky playing cards into the crowd? Those were good times.

On the trip to see my dad, Kate rode up front with my mom, and I got in the back so I could have my own seat-back screen. Plus, Kate didn't give me a choice.

I went to sleep as soon as we left, and I woke up when Kate and my mom started arguing in the front seat. "Why would you pack *carrots*?" said Kate, who was looking through the snacks. "If you're going to make me eat, you should at least be considerate. I notice *you* aren't eating a whole bunch of carrots."

"Kate," said my mom. "Just eat something. Anything. You don't need to eat the carrots. There are radishes. There's hummus. Cherries. How about an egg?"

"Oh my god!" shrieked Kate. "Hummus? An egg? Ugh."

"I can't win," muttered my mom.

I put my headphones on and started watching Dakota Roche videos. He's this hardcore rider. He shows his wipeouts and radical tricks that would definitely kill me if I tried them. I forgot to mention before that on Friday Ben asked if I wanted to go for a ride on Sunday. I said sure, even though I don't have a bike. If you're going to make friends, you have to extend yourself. You know, Rule #5: Put Together a Winning Team.

When we got into city traffic near Las Vegas after about four hours, I started to pay more attention. We turned into a new subdivision and stopped behind a building surrounded with a lot of cacti. There was a fountain near the front door.

Mom shut off the ignition and turned to us.

"I have no idea how this is going to go," she said. "Let's just do our best, okay?"

My sister snorted. "*We're* not the ones who need to do our best," she said. "Maybe Daddy should have thought of that—"

"That's enough, Kate," said my mom. "Now is *not* the time."

36

I opened the door, but before I could get out, Mom gestured at me to take off my headphones.

"I can hear," I said.

"Please leave your devices in the car."

"But then how is he going to tune everything out?" asked my sister.

Heat is bad for electronics. Also, someone could break in and take them. This seemed like a nice neighborhood, but there could still be criminals wandering around. It was Las Vegas, after all. Everyone probably needed money to gamble. I said all that to my mom.

"Here," she said and held out her hand. "If you don't want to leave them in the car, I'll put them in my purse."

Then she grabbed a big carry-all bag from the back of the car.

My mom pressed the buzzer at the front door and it was opened by a tall man with no hair. He had very high cheekbones and smooth, dark skin. He looked sort of like a movie star.

He said hello and asked us in. The place had a front desk, like a hotel, and there was a wall with water running down it and lots of white chairs with pillows. I was worried the place was going to look like a hospital, but it was actually nice. That was good. My dad's into nice things and he'll probably feel better sooner in a place like this.

My mom followed the bald man to the counter and they talked for a while. I was looking around, sort of taking it in, like you're supposed to do if you're a writer. In one corner a man was talking to a woman who sat across from him. She was crying. I looked away. I hate to see people violating Rule #3. Anyone who cries while visiting someone at a treatment center is definitely showing their unlucky hand.

Kate tugged on my arm. "Come on," she said. "We have to get searched."

I actually thought she was joking.

"Don't be a dummy. You can't just walk in here. You have to get checked for contraband." I could tell she loved saying the word "contraband" and knowing that I didn't know what it meant.

Kate was wearing her old-man pants and a checked yellow blouse with puffy sleeves, and her hair was lumpy. She looked pretty contraband-y, if you ask me, especially if contraband means terrible. She was also too pale from lack of carbs.

"Rodney, come over here please," said my mom. She had on a dress and her black hair was down and curly, the way my dad always tells her he likes it. That was interesting. I guess she doesn't totally hate him.

"Can you come into this room over here, little man?" asked the big guy who opened the door.

"Little man," snickered my sister.

We walked into a small room with four chairs and a table and nothing else. It smelled like new carpet. We could see outside into a courtyard. It was filled with outdoor tables and chairs and tons of plants and two more fountains, which was an impressive number of fountains, even for Vegas.

"Please put your belongings here," said the man, pointing at the table.

My mom put her purse and the big bag on the table and the man pulled on gloves and started to go through all her stuff.

"Ewww," said my sister. "He's not touching my things."

I thought the man would get mad, because she was being rude, but he didn't. "It's for everyone's safety," he said, his voice calm, "including your dad's."

Kate went quiet after that.

We pulled out our pockets and he said he wouldn't pat us down. "We're not San Quentin," he said.

"Not unless San Quentin costs thirty thousand dollars a month now," muttered my mom.

The man must have heard her, but he pretended he didn't.

Instead, he led us down a hallway with a lot of doors.

"I'll bring you to your husband. He's just finishing up with some other visitors, but I know he's excited to see you all."

He opened a door to a big TV room where my dad sat by himself in front of a card table. My half sister and half brother stood near the door like they were on their way out.

"Oh good," said my half sister, who is twenty-one. "The nanny and her kids are here. That's perfect, Dad. Icing on the cupcake."

You've never met her, but my half sister, Cardi, looks like the complete opposite of my sister. She wears a lot of makeup and has long bright-blonde Disney mermaid hair and wears tight clothes. But she's also kind of mean, so I guess in that way, you can sort of tell they're related. Yates is tall and has normal blond hair and he smiles a lot.

"Hello, Cardi," said my mom, who always says she wasn't just their nanny before she and my dad got together. She also taught them family fitness and yoga.

When anyone mentions how she used to work for my dad, my mom says at least she's *had* a job in the past, which is more than Cardi and Yates's mother can say. My dad calls her his most expensive mistake. And I guess us children of divorce have to get exposed to some negativity. As you know, I don't see my half brother and half sister. When Dad goes to visit them, he doesn't bring us, and they have never been to our house. It's too bad because I like Yates. He's nineteen and has developmental delays and we get along. He's really easygoing, and I think that must run in the boys in our family because it sure doesn't run in the girls.

Cardi made a barfing noise and pulled Yates out of the room.

"Bye, you guys," he said.

Kate ignored him, but my mom and I waved. "Bye, Yates," I said.

My mom's mouth was a straight line and her nostrils were flaring, which meant she was upset. She's usually a very calm person, but she really hates it when Cardi calls her the nanny. Sometimes she tells my dad that his friends look down on her because of how she used to be a family fitness nanny, but he always tells her that some of his best friends' wives and husbands used to be worse than that, and that in Vegas it doesn't matter what you used to be as long as you look good now, which she does. I still remember your mom telling him to never say that again once she overheard him. Maybe it's because your mom is from Georgia. Things are probably different there. Fewer rude British poker players. Ha. Ha.

"Hello, darlings," said my dad, like nothing had happened. "It is so good to see you."

You know how my dad seems sort of young for an older person? I also think he's handsome for his age, even though he's not skinny. Well, he was looking old even for an older person. It was sort of a shock.

My sister and mom just stood there, but I went and gave him a big hug. He got out of his chair and hugged me back. "Rodney," he said.

Then he invited us to sit around the small table. I sat right down, and for a minute, I thought my mom and my sister were going to keep standing. If someone invites you to sit, you should really do it. Finally, they sat down, but they didn't hug him, which was awkward.

He did that thing where he looked into each of our faces. "Well, well, well," he said. "Isn't this a caution?"

"That's one word for it," said my mom. "I brought you some of the snacks you asked for." She shoved the big bag across the counter.

"You're a saint," he said.

"Apparently," she agreed. "I put in a box of that tea you like."

"Not just a saint, but also a goddess," he said.

Kate sighed. "I'm enjoying this so much," she muttered. "Please let it be over soon."

"Kate?" My dad was looking at her. Remember how he and Kate used to joke around? And how they have the same sense of humor and he always said she had her own style and voice, which was rare for a girl her age? I think he was trying to be positive about how she is, which is kind of . . . well, unpleasant and not quite normal or whatever. And remember he taught her poker even though mom said no cards and no gambling until we're twenty-one? Remember how we were jealous, at least I was, especially since *we* were the ones living by the Lucky Life Rules, and Kate said they were a gambling version of toxic positivity, whatever that is?

"Yes, Father," said Kate.

"You seem pretty angry."

"You think?" she said.

"Is there something you'd like to say?" he asked.

Kate's eyes were all wet and she was sort of vibrating, like someone had given her an electric shock. "How could you?" she said.

My dad looked down, and my mom put her hand over her mouth.

"I read about what you did to Missy Steph—"

"Can I be excused?" I said. I needed to use the bathroom. And I didn't want to hear about how Kate is angry again or about the movie star who ruined our lives.

"No!" said Kate. "You can stay here and listen."

"If he needs to go to the bathroom," said my mom.

"Kate, you shouldn't believe everything you read in the media," said my dad. "The center has offered to get us a counselor to discuss all this. To help us get through this rough patch. But I said no. We can handle this alone. As a family."

"Will the counselor also make excuses for you?" said Kate.

"I really have to go," I said. I actually did. The conversation was upsetting my stomach. I know you get it because of your thing with dairy.

"If twerp gets to leave, so do I," said Kate. "This sucks."

"Kate, you have to understand that I'm doing what I need to do for my health," said my dad.

She made a kind of screeching noise, like a bird whose egg just got stolen by a rat. "Your health?" said Kate. "Your reputation, more like. What about the wome—"

"Oh god," said my mom. "I don't think I can do this. Jeremy, you and I need to discuss this alone. Let's leave the kids out of it for now." She was crying. It was awful. Almost as bad as our family meeting.

"So you're willing to speak to me?" asked my dad, and he was completely breaking the rule about never showing what you want.

"I think I'm going to use the bathroom too," said my mom, which was odd because she doesn't like using strange bathrooms.

"Me too," said Kate.

"Me three!" I said, because it was usually just the three of us doing stuff because my dad wasn't at home much. It's sort of a joke in our family, mostly just between me and Mom because Kate never thinks it's funny and just rolls her eyes when one of us says it.

"You guys are just walking away? Leaving me here?" My dad was trying to sound like he was making a joke, but he was upset.

"No, Dad," I said. "I'll wait until they get back."

My mom and sister left the little room, and my dad asked me about what shows I'd been watching on TV and about how school was going, but he didn't seem too interested in my answers. It seemed like he was just waiting to be sure my mom and sister were really gone so he could ask about them.

"Are they okay, Champ?" he asked. "Emotionally, I mean. They've had so many changes in such a short time. With the move and everything."

I shrugged. I'd had a lot of changes too. There was no way I was going to tell him that they fought constantly about Kate not eating and my mom not smiling and worrying about money, and how my new school was full of old guy–looking kids and kids with emotional problems and braids wrapped around their heads like crowns, and how I missed you and the rest of my friends and our house and Circle Square School and him. Especially him.

"They're okay, I guess."

"It's just temporary," he said. "I've got to work through some things. Get some clarity. Get right with myself. And make a few amends for the misunderstandings."

I nodded.

"A word of advice, if you'll allow me," he said. "Don't pay attention to what's in the media. Some people are looking for attention. Exaggerating. You know who I am. You know me."

I took a deep breath and nodded. He was right. He was my dad and I knew him better than anyone. And I liked him better than anyone too.

"It's okay, Dad," I said. "It'll be okay."

"Oh, Rodney, you were always such a sensitive kid."

"Yeah, I think I better go to the bathroom too." I got up and went out the door. My mom was waiting in the hallway in front of a door marked Women. I could hear water running inside.

"Kate's been in there a long time," said my mom. "Should I knock?"

That was a weird thing for her to ask. I'm the kid. How was I supposed to know what she should do?

"I guess."

Mom knocked on the door. "Kate?" she called.

Kate didn't answer.

"Are you okay in there?" asked my mom.

Now some doors opened in the hallway and people looked out of their rooms. I wondered which ones were here for drugs and alcohol and gambling and which ones were here for misunderstandings. Not to be rude, but it was hard to tell. They all looked like they were in for all of it.

"Kate? Kate?" My mom's voice was getting louder. "You better not be throwing up in there!"

"*Mom*," I said, because that was pretty embarrassing and I knew Kate wouldn't like it AT ALL.

The water stopped and Kate threw the door open.

"MOM!" she screamed. "I CAN'T BELIEVE YOU WOULD SAY THAT!"

Now almost all the doors in the hallway were open, but I noticed my dad didn't come out of our meeting room. The tall guy from the reception area and a gray-haired lady with a badge on a lanyard around her neck came toward us.

45

"I'm just going to use this bathroom over here," I said, even though no one was listening to me.

Once I was in the bathroom with the door locked, I tried not to listen, but I could hear my mom yelling and my sister yelling and a lady saying something about taking a breath.

Then it went quiet again. Maybe they all went back in to see my dad. Maybe they left. I sat on the toilet seat and stared at the floor.

I didn't hear anything for a long time, like at least five minutes or more, and then someone knocked on the bathroom door. I actually texted you then, but you were probably busy.

"Hello? Rodney?" A man's voice. Maybe it was the big guy from the front.

"Yes?" I said. I felt like I was floating in space. No body. No plans. Just nothing. It was okay actually.

"You done in there?"

"Yeah," I said.

"You want to come out?"

I didn't, but I also didn't like to say that. Until we left, I never appreciated all the bathrooms in our old house. Our new house has one plain little bathroom, and I can hardly ever get in there because my mom and sister are always using it. So I figured I should take my time in this one. It was clean and quiet.

There were cactus and flower shapes pressed into the tiles, which was nice.

"Rodney? Is your stomach okay?" My mom's voice.

"It's fine."

Then I got up and unlocked the door. The reception guy and my mom and the lady with the long gray hair piled on her head stood outside.

"Oh, baby," said my mom. She had been crying. Again.

"I know your father wanted to have this initial meeting with you on his own, but I think it would be helpful if we facilitated," said the lady.

My mom looked like someone had squished all the shine and fun out of her. "My daughter is waiting outside in the car. I don't think we'll be visiting any more today," she said.

"I understand. We'll make a plan for the next time. We want to develop healthy lines of communication."

The lady was dressed in a long gray dress and it made me feel calmer just to look at her. She was a cloud lady. Cool and calm in this dark hallway with the little lights hidden in the walls and soft carpets under our feet.

"My name is Elizabeth," said the woman. "We'll all meet together next time, Rodney." I wasn't sure how she knew my name.

"Sure," I said. I liked talking to her. I almost always like talking to people or at least listening to people talk. It's more fun than thinking my own thoughts. Next time we came to visit my dad, I would find people to talk to. People who are not in my family. If you're free, I could maybe FaceTime you or something.

My mom had her giant purse over one shoulder and the bag she'd brought to my dad was empty. He still hadn't come out of the little room. Maybe he was in there watching TV.

"We'll be in touch," said the woman, Elizabeth, as my mom and I walked down the hallway.

"Thank you," said my mom.

She didn't look back at the meeting room, but I did. The door didn't open. My dad didn't come out. The ride home sucked rocks.

So that's my story.

I hope you get in touch soon. I want to know how your first week of school went. Oh, and if I was sending this, which I'm not, I'd tell you to say hi to your mom for me.

Rodney

7

Hey, Lar,

So you know how you always say I'm too cautious to ever make it to the top level in *Death Spawn*? Well, I might be getting bolder. I think you'll be impressed when you hear about today. Level 72, baby! I'm coming for your crown. So here's what happened.

Ben showed up at our house at, like, eight in the morning. Eight! On a Sunday!

"Rodney," said my mom. "There's someone hopping around on his bike in front of the house. Where is that boy's helmet?"

I told her he was here for me. I'd been ready since half past seven because I was kind of nervous about biking and because I heard somewhere that adventure people are also morning people. I wore my gym shorts and sneakers and a T-shirt. They seemed like the best clothes for doing sports outside. If I fell, at least I wouldn't wreck my good clothes. I might not get any more now that we're broke.

My mom asked why he didn't come to the door and asked again where his helmet was.

"Because he's a freak," said my sister. It was the first thing she'd said since the day before. She'd just come out of her bedroom to get coffee. Carbs = 0.

"We're going out," I said.

"What? Where?" asked my mom.

She wasn't used to me having things to do or leaving the house. You know, back home I mostly hung out by the pool.

"Out," I told her, which felt pretty hardcore.

"Ha!" said my sister. "Out! What are you? A sixteen-year-old girl? What kind of eleven-year-old says that?"

"Kate," said my mom.

"Well, really," said Kate. "Even at my worst I don't just say 'out.' I give you a proper lie to set your mind at ease. I must have learned how to do that from our dear old—"

"Enough!" said my mother.

I didn't point out that Kate never goes out either, especially since we moved here. Back home she hung out with Lav and Cav. You remember them. My sister's best friends? The ones who also dress like old men and only smile after they say something rude or listen to sad music or read one of their depressing poems on the internet.

If you don't remember, Cavendish is the one who is trying to be an Instagram poet, but so far, it's mostly just Lavender and Kate who follow her. You know more about poetry than I do, but I don't think hers is going to be popular because it doesn't even rhyme and nothing good ever happens in it. To be honest, it's always surprising to me that she can read the poems because she wears her hair right in front of her eyes when she goes on camera. Maybe she has the poems memorized.

Remember how they would sit by the pool under the umbrella while wearing huge hats and long sleeves, talking about how much they hated the sun?

"I think we're going hiking. Or biking."

"Where?" asked my mom. "And who *is* that?"

"His name is Ben."

"Ben who? Can I meet his parents?"

"We're just going over there," I said, and pointed to the trail behind the house.

"Alone?"

"Together," I said.

"It's fine, Mom," said Kate. "We won't miss him anyway. He eats too much and is kind of a suck-up."

"Kate!" said my mother.

"When will you be home?" she asked me.

"An hour," I said. "Or two."

"This seems dangerous. Please bring your phone. And text me every half hour. No, every fifteen minutes."

"Seriously?" said Kate.

"I'll text," I said. "Don't worry. I'll be fine. He's in my class. He's nice."

"No getting on anything with wheels without a helmet!" she said.

I slipped out the front door before she could say any more. I still can't quite believe she let me go without even phoning his folks.

When I got out there, Ben asked where my bike was, and I had to tell him I didn't have one.

"Okay. We can go to my place and I'll get you set up. I'll double you there." That kind of freaked me out.

I looked back at my house. I could see my mom and sister standing in the little front window. Watching. It felt like an Instant Pot pressure cooker situation for sure. I was caught between my mother and a hard spot!

Ben asked if there was a problem, and I had to tell him I couldn't get on a bike without a helmet. Or a skateboard, or a scooter, or anything except my runners. But I only said about the bike.

"Right," he said. He looked over at my mom and sister. He waved and my mom waved back. My sister just stared. "We'll get out of sight first."

We walked together down the sidewalk and onto the trail. Then we followed the trail back behind our house and onto the street behind ours. And when we hit the road, he told me to get on. Dangerous as heck, and I did it anyway! He got me to stand on the pegs and I had to hold onto his shoulders, which felt sort of weird but also interesting because I didn't even know some bikes have pegs. Also, he rode off the curb a bunch of times, so I had to stay extremely alert.

It was uncomfortable, but I also felt like an outlaw biker with the wind going through my hair, not that I would say that to anyone except you. Have you ever got on a bike or a skateboard or Rollerblades without a helmet? I have to say that it feels different, maybe because it's so irresponsible. He pedaled in front of me, so I guess that would make me like one of those outlaw biker girlfriends who ride on the back of the motorcycle, based on what

I've seen on the TV shows about biker gangs. Kate hates those shows and asks why anyone would want to watch hairy guys acting like sexist pigs. She doesn't understand the call of the wild and the open road.

We rode for about ten minutes and stopped at a trailer just off this little road. There were no other houses around. There were three old trucks painted neat colors like turquoise and pinky-red and yellow parked outside and a washing machine and dryer on the covered porch. A newer truck with a camper on it sat next to the old trucks. The only trailer I'd ever been in was on the set of a few TV shows or movies when my dad was doing a guest spot. Remember that time we got to go in the trailer of that hilarious actress who makes that face? She was so nice to give us all that candy. Too bad my dad didn't get the recurring role the way she said he might.

Ben told me to wait outside.

Then this guy came out. He was sort of short and thin, but he had a lot of muscles and long black hair tied up on the top of his head.

"Hi, I'm Rodney," I said. Normally I would shake hands with new people, like you're supposed to, but the guy wasn't exactly like an adult, because he was too cool. So I just didn't do anything.

"You here for Ben?"

I nodded.

The guy disappeared into the trailer again and yelled, "Ben! There's someone here to see you! Get up!"

Then another guy who looked almost exactly the same as the first one appeared in the doorway, but this one had short hair. I blinked to make sure my eyes hadn't gone strange.

"Hey," said the second one. The two of them were probably around twenty.

"Ben's not here," said the second one.

"Yes, I am," said Ben, coming around the corner pushing a bike. I realized that he looked like a smaller version of the guys in the doorway. They came onto the porch, and they didn't have shirts on, and with all their muscles and tattoos, they looked extremely tough, and I felt extremely Circle Square School, if you get what I'm saying.

"Where you guys going?" asked one.

"Thought we'd go up Snuff Hill," said Ben.

"Can your friend ride?"

I froze. No. No, I wasn't, and I didn't like the name of the hill. It was a bad name. I'm aware that when it's used as a verb, to "snuff" means to kill someone. "Ben, what are you thinking?" said the other twin. He nodded at me. "I'm Greg. The most safety-conscious of the Yamamoto-Whitman clan."

"As if," said the other one. "You broke four bones last year. I only broke two and Ben one."

"I break bones so you don't have to," said Greg.

"My dad broke six bones last year," said Ben. "Left forearm, right big toe, hairline fracture of the left femur, and I forget the rest."

They all laughed like it was so funny. My eyes were bugging out of my head. What kind of terrible thing was happening in their family?

"He broke them all in one accident, so it doesn't totally count. I'm Jiro, by the way."

54

"Dude, you can't take him on Snuff. Everyone eats it on that trail. So steep you're sucking wind the whole way up and full of logs and skinnies on the way down," said the one called Greg.

"Fine. We'll go to the gorge, then."

Before anyone could say anything, an older man came out of the house. He was yawning and wearing boxer shorts. I looked away. I wasn't used to people's parents wandering around in underpants. I also wasn't used to people talking about all their broken bones.

"Guys, you know I worked until three. I'm soloing Golden Boy this afternoon at two o'clock when the winds should be less spicy. I've got my chute, but I don't want to have to use it. I need some more shut-eye. So how about you keep it down out here?"

I didn't understand anything he said, but it all sounded super cool.

"Sorry, Pops," said all three of the brothers at the same time. But they didn't seem afraid of him, and he didn't seem angry or anything.

Then he noticed me.

"Hello," he said.

"Hi. I'm Rodney." I said that because it didn't seem like Ben was going to introduce me. My mom would have a kitten if I didn't introduce my friends properly.

"It's nice to meet you, Rodney. You going riding with Ben?"

Ben nodded.

"That's great. You guys have fun, eh."

Then he went back inside. No questions about where we were going, when we'd be back, whether we had sunscreen on, how often we'd text, whether we'd packed a nutritious lunch or even any water. Ben lived like a wild animal, compared to me. It was really impressive as well as aspirational, which I think is what it's called when you want something. These guys seemed like they probably followed all the Rules for Living a Lucky Life just naturally.

I put on the helmet Ben handed me. It had the cool face mask part, so I felt like a horror villain, which was awesome, even if it was sort of stinky inside the helmet and probably not too hygienic. I wanted to take a picture of myself to send you, but Ben didn't seem much like a selfie guy and taking one would make me look uncool, so I didn't do it. If I go again, I'll take one when Ben isn't looking.

He'd wheeled two other bikes out from behind the trailer. They weren't BMXs, which was okay with me, since they only have one gear and if you're out of shape I think you need a lot of gears. I wondered what else was back there. I bet it was all adventure stuff, like trampolines with no safety nets, slingshots and slacklines, dirt bikes and snowboards, and probably outlawed fireworks.

The bike had knobby tires and was pretty comfortable when I sat on it.

"Do you need to adjust the seat?" asked Ben.

"No," I said, because I was too embarrassed to admit that I didn't know if the height was right.

"Thought we'd take mountain bikes. No need for downhill bikes if we're just going to the gorge."

"How many bikes do you have?" I asked.

He shrugged. "I dunno. Between all of us, maybe eighteen or twenty?"

"Oh," I said, because what else do you say to something like that. For some reason I felt luckier than I'd ever felt before. Even more than when my dad won that huge championship game before he retired and the newspapers took pictures of him and us.

Ben got on his bike, which was bigger than his BMX, hit a dirt jump, got some major air, and we pedaled away. I felt free. No one could see who I was, and anything could happen. It was awesome, even when I got tired, which I did after about ten minutes because I think I game too much.

But I tried to keep up. We went past the school and Ben jumped his bike down some stairs, only he called it "gapping," and then we rode past a few big stores on the edge of town and onto the main highway out of town. That felt pretty dangerous even though it's just two lanes. Cars zoomed past and a few times the wind nearly knocked me over. Ben did tricks the whole time. The guy never just rides straight. Maybe that's why he's so good.

We turned onto a side road that was paved at first and then turned to dirt. It went up over a low hill, more of a lump, really, and then down. Ben stopped his bike on a bridge that crossed a narrow river way below.

"Is this the gorge?" I asked.

"Nah," he said. Then he headed down a narrow, winding trail that ran along the edge of the river, through some trees. The path was sandy and rutted. Puffs of dust followed us. The trees looked kind of dried up and dead. I followed him and tried not to look over the edge into the river below. One fall and you'd end up falling down the bank into the water. Ben hit a jump coming out of a turn, flew into the air, and disappeared down the trail. If he'd landed a foot to the side he'd have ended up way below in the river.

When I caught up with him he had stopped, and his bike was leaned against one of the scrawny, dusty trees.

"That's the gorge," he said and pointed down. Below us—like way, way below us—was a pool of water. There were rock ledges sticking out all the way down. I hoped he wasn't suggesting that we—

"We're going to jump," he said.

You would have freaked, Larry. It was the least safe activity I've ever seen, never mind tried. Worse than those bike videos I've been watching.

At first, I hoped that I heard him wrong.

"Like from lower down?" I said.

"Nah, that's for wusses," said Ben. "We jump like men!"

I looked at him. He was my size, but skinnier from doing so much physical activity and having a dad who didn't seem into eating. Ben wanted to act like a man. I wanted to act like a . . . well, someone who liked being alive so he could play games and watch stuff and eat pot pies. If being a man meant risking my life by jumping off a cliff, I would give that a hard pass, which is what my dad used to say when he really didn't want to do something, which, now that I think about it, was actually quite a few things.

All I said was "oh."

"Don't worry," said Ben. "Hardly anyone has died doing it."

I stared at him. I thought he was joking. "I don't have my swim stuff," I said. I didn't mention that I liked to go out to the pool with my scuba mask and swim fins and that we used to float around on huge floaties shaped like flamingos and slices of pizza.

"Bare ass it!" he said. "Live free!"

I had never once thought about bare-assing it. Imagine my sister and her friends, sitting under the umbrella in their big hats, watching, disgusted, as we swam around naked in our pool. My dad might have done it, but that's because he's English. And he wouldn't have done that in front of my sister and her friends. At least, I hope not.

"It's a rush. You're going to love it," Ben said. And then he took off his shirt and his baggy biking pants that were half shorts and half pants, and his dirty shoes. He had faded swim trunks underneath. He walked out to the edge of the rock, and without saying one more word, he jumped off the edge. He didn't even scream as he fell. All I heard was the splash.

Eventually, I got up the nerve to go near the edge. Ben was waving up at me from the water.

Oh no. I'm telling you, Larry, I didn't want new friends enough to do it.

"Come on!" He was so far down I could hardly hear him.

Even though I knew I wasn't going to jump because that would be crazy, I took off my shirt and shoes. I left my socks on because I was definitely not going to do it.

Next thing I knew I was standing at the edge of the cliff. My heart bashed around in my chest, and I thought I might be having an anxiety attack, even though I'm so easygoing. I took off my socks. None of the rules covered this. Maybe #2: Look for the Upside? Or was it

59

#10: Avoid the Negative? There was no rule that said real men do death-defying jumps.

I got this rushing noise in my ears and my legs were numb. But I also felt like nothing mattered, which made the decision easier.

So I jumped. On the way down, something touched my back. Bumped it. But I couldn't think about it because I hit the water feet-first and it felt like smacking into something solid. I went down, down, down until my heels hit the bottom of the river. My breath stopped from the cold and I thought maybe my heart stopped too. Then I swam up, and it was like my body didn't even need me anymore. It had its own life. When I came out of the water, I felt ten times more alive and it was amazing.

"Dude!" shouted Ben. He'd swum up to me so he was right in my face. "Are you okay?"

"Yeah," I said.

"You were so close to the edge. I thought you hit something. You sure you're okay?"

"Sure," I said. But when we got out of the water, I felt something warm on my back, and when I felt it, my hand came away all covered in blood.

Ben was all excited. "You're injured. Awesome."

I didn't think it was awesome at all, but it was cool that he thought it was.

"Yeah," I said, like I meant to hit a big rock ledge on the way down.

"Want to go again?"

"Naw," I said. At first the water in the river seemed warm, but then it turned freezing. I'm not sure why. "I've got to text my mom and get back." I could feel myself starting to shake.

We climbed out of the water and started making our way up the steep bank. When we got to the top, I noticed a wooden cross with some plastic flowers on it.

"What's that?"

"It's for a girl who died."

"From jumping?" I asked.

"Yeah. I think she hit her head on a ledge."

I nearly threw up.

All of a sudden, I wasn't numb anymore, or cold. My legs were all wobbly and my ears were ringing.

I nearly died! Just like the girl.

"Yeah, and another kid got paralyzed a few years ago. Hit his back on the way down."

I could hardly see. I thought I was going to pass out. Why had I been so crazy? Why did Ben risk our lives like that?

"You've got to be careful when you jump here. Can't panic. And you can't let anyone catch you jumping. They keep talking about building a fence, but they never do." Ben looked at me. "You okay, man?" he asked.

"Yeah," I said.

He slapped me on the back. He didn't hit the part that was bleeding, but it still hurt because my whole body felt bruised.

"Do your brothers jump here? And your dad? Is that how you learned?"

"Not really. Both of my parents and my brothers do stunts for videos and movies, mostly bike stuff. We come here sometimes to cool off. This is just jumping in a river. It's not that hard. Don't worry. The first time is always the scariest."

I was pretty sure there wasn't going to be a second time, but I didn't say that.

When we rode back to his house, I felt like I'd gone on one of those carnival rides that spins you around and around so you feel like you're spinning even when it's over. I think I was in shock.

When I got off the mountain bike, he made me show my back to his brothers, and they made faces.

"Little dude," said Jiro. "Close call."

"Not really," I said. Even though it was THE CLOSEST CALL EVER! But with these guys, I had to keep playing like it was no big deal.

"Ben, you got to be careful with your friends," said Greg. "He coulda got hurt."

Still, I think they were impressed.

"You should have seen our mom jump in that bad boy," said Jiro. "She did a backflip. We got video."

"Is your mom home?" I asked Ben. I really wanted to meet a mom who would backflip into that gorge.

Ben's face went dark. "Nah," he said. "She's not here."

"She'll be back, little man," said Greg, putting his hand on Ben's shoulder. "Not too many who can do what she does. Lots of demand for her skills."

"Is she a stuntwoman?" I asked.

"That's right. Best in the business," said Jiro. "Learned back home in Squamish, where people know how to push the line. She's there now. In Canada."

"Oh," I said.

All three brothers stopped talking, and I didn't ask any more questions because people sometimes like privacy. After all, I wasn't about to tell them that my dad was in a treatment center because a movie star didn't like to be hugged.

When I got home, I went into my room really fast so my mom wouldn't see that my shirt was bloody at the back.

I closed the door and stood in the narrow space between my bed and the wall with the Ant-Man mirror on it. The mirror is cool because it has three sections. In one you look really small, in one you look big, and in one you look regular. I took off my shirt and twisted around so I could see. Even in the reflection where I was small, my back looked bad. It was turning purple and a strip of skin was peeled off and the skin underneath was red.

I put my shirt in a bag and put it under my bed so I could throw it out at school. Then I put on a dark T-shirt before I put on another shirt over top of it in case I started bleeding again.

Maybe I nearly died, but at least I had a new friend who was from a stunt family. If you come to visit, I think you'll like Ben. But you'll probably be smart enough not to jump. You know, sometimes I think I'd rather not be alive than not have friends. Do you ever feel that way? Probably not. It's probably just me.

Take care, Lar.

Stay on the bank!

Rodney

8

Hey, Larry,

I haven't written for a while because things were going better here. Until they weren't. Maybe you heard about it. In case you didn't, here's what happened. After I jumped in the river, Ben told everyone about it and people started coming up to me asking to see my back. It was one big bruise and it killed to move for a few days, but I pretended that I hardly felt anything.

Our school only has about two hundred kids and a surprising number of them are elite athletes, including Ben! He's been in a bunch of videos, mostly doing free-style with his brothers. He's sponsored by GearX, which is this independent bike company. His dad and brothers have big-name sponsors. They all get lots of free stuff to wear and ride. In the other sixth-grade class there are two girls who are climbers. All those athlete-type kids are popular, or they would be if they went to school more. Ben says they have to miss a lot of days because they're at climbing and biking competitions. He said the older kids are sponsored, which I think is like when an actor promotes a product, like perfume or jewelry or cars, only the athlete kids advertise outdoor clothes and bikes and equipment. I should see if I can get sponsored by Mrs. Perfect Pies. Or peas. Anyway, the point is that adventurous people are impressed when you get injured doing dangerous things, so jumping off the cliff and nearly dying was my best social move so far.

Ben has only been at Stony Butte for a year and a half because his family moves around a lot to do stunts, so he's pretty new here too.

The day after the jump, Dave and Macii and Rigmor came over to where I was eating lunch alone. When Ben's actually at school, he goes to the bike park on his break. They said they were sorry for bailing on me when Chum came over to beat me up. They said they'd learned that it was best to avoid Chum when he got mad like that. I said I understood and that they probably shouldn't call him Chum because he doesn't like it and would instead like to be called Fisherman.

Then they invited me to hang out with them, and I got to talk to Rigmor, which was excellent.

What's even more surprising is that Fisherman and I are sort of getting to be friends now. It's hard to say if a person is technically your friend if you have to worry he will break your arm if you say the wrong thing. But he says hi and doesn't menace me. I also don't say much when I see him just in case I make him mad again.

At the end of school a few days ago, he came over to me and asked if I was having any problems with anyone. I said no. And he said that was good and he looked sort of mad at the thought of me having problems, which I appreciated.

Classes here are a lot easier than at Circle Square, and while I'm not exactly popular, I haven't been used as a battering ram since the first time. So that's good.

Rigmor told me her brother manages the local comics and games store, which I was happy to hear about because I didn't even know there was one in town. She said we could go there after school one day and I could meet her brother. That was something I didn't even have back home! Could anything be better than being friends with a girl who practically owns her own comic-book store? No.

Things were so good that I almost started to like Stony Butte Elementary for a while there. I was feeling so good I sent you a couple of texts and a game invite. I wondered if you were missing me and didn't know what to say. But you didn't reply. Again. That made me glad I'd already decided not to send this. Unless you really want to read it when we're back in touch and things are normal again.

I wonder if people are only your friends when you can see them in person. If so, why is my sister constantly talking to her mopey friends from back home about how sad they all are and how no one understands them? Why isn't anyone talking to me? I started worrying about you and your mom. I wondered if you guys were having money troubles since the TV show is shut down. When we had our bad family meeting, my dad said your mom was "another factor." I didn't know what that meant. He felt bad about everyone who worked on the show losing their jobs. My dad cares about people. He really does.

Never mind. Back to the good stuff. My mom and I were making things happen at Stony Butt, which is what I call this town in my mind, but I don't say it out loud because I don't want my mom or anyone else to think I'm making fun of this place. My mom has a new job and she just got asked to teach a Pilates class at the community center. I saw my sister reading a book that didn't have a black cover with a bat or a vampire on it. Everything was looking up. Or almost everything. At least for a while.

This past Monday, Ben rode me home on his bike and said we should go rock climbing, which sounded terrible and dangerous, but I was still glad to be asked. Rigmor invited me to go to her brother's store, which I was excited and also sort of nervous about.

On Tuesday, my mom and sister and I had dinner, and my sister and my mom actually ate some beans, which meant they both got in a better mood almost right away because of how carbs bring the joy. We even laughed a couple of times. Those were the first laughs we had in that house. I played games online with Dave and Macii and Rigmor.

Then Wednesday happened.

After I did my homework, which was to make a diorama showing the layers of the ocean floor, I went online to watch Van Johnson like I do every night. You'll be surprised to hear that even people at Stony Butte like him. I know your mom thinks he's incredibly dumb and that he needs a parent to step in and give him some rules because of how he trashes his basement with his bike and skateboard and spray paint and everything. Why do

68

grown-ups only notice that stuff and not how he makes hilarious songs and plays guitar and has awesome hair and jokes? Obviously my dad appreciated him, since he was a guest on Van Johnson's show and Van Johnson went on *Get Lucky*, even though he's underage. Remember how mad your mom was after they taped that episode? How she said Van Johnson was a terrible role model for young men? That was it for you watching Van Johnson, at least when your mom was around.

Anyway, I had on my Van Johnson T-shirt when I sat down to watch. It was new song Wednesday. Graffiti in his basement on Thursdays. Pranks on Fridays. Stunts on Saturdays. Gaming on Sundays. Small explosions Mondays. Tuesdays off. For a wild man YouTuber, he's pretty organized. He reminds me of you that way, but that's definitely all you have in common with him. I mean, you're always pretty decent to people. Van Johnson: not so much.

Anyway, I was stoked for the song. I clicked on his channel and there he was, livestreaming. You know how you always say his hair looks like a blond cat sitting on his head? Well, it looked extra catlike on Wednesday.

If you haven't watched the video because you're not allowed, Van started out staring into the camera from his trashed basement. Considering he's so rich, he should be able to afford to fix some of the scorch marks and the skateboard jumps. He and his friends Ned and Blister somehow attached a couch to the wall about two feet off the ground. The episode when they did that was hilarious but also incredibly dumb. That's why I watch. I just want to hang out with them and see what they'll do next. I'm not very mature, obviously.

"It pains me to sing this," said Van.

Ned and Blister, who were sitting on a broken loveseat off to the side and behind him, nodded. It must be strange to spend your whole life just watching your famous friend. I wonder if they ever get annoyed with him? He's not that nice, like when he makes Ned do stuff and Ned gets hurt, and when he forces Blister to say what girl he likes and call her up to tell her and it's obvious she doesn't like Blister back. Ugh. I'm glad our friendship isn't like that. At least, it wasn't, back when we talked.

"For real. This next one is about someone I know. And someone you know." He put his hand on his chest, like his heart was sore, except he put it on the wrong side, so it wasn't really on his heart, but closer to his superior vena cava, which is this blood vessel that takes blood to the heart and which I learned about back when I went to a proper school. Sorry. That was sort of a downer.

I was like, *here we go!* Whenever Van Johnson starts a song talking about how bad he feels, it's going to be a good one. The worse he feels, the meaner the song.

"But you got to call people on their stuff, am I right?" Ned and Blister nodded.

"We're juvenile delinquents, but even we wouldn't pull this kind of stuff, man. We respect the females."

More nodding from Ned and Blister.

"Especially good-looking ones," said Van. Then he bent his head, so all you could see was the top of his fluffy hair. He strummed his guitar, and Ned and Blister got out their

70

little bongo drums. They didn't sit up straight or anything. They just play sideways on that crooked couch.

He started singing. At first, I was nodding along because it sounded just like that Elton John song my parents used to play all the time. He sang:

> *I slimed a girl again last night on set*
> *From nine to zero hours five p.m.*
> *And I'm gonna be all hands by ten.*
> *I miss my wife and kids so much I got to mack*
> *On even famous babes.*

I stopped nodding.

> *And I think it's gonna be a long, long time*
> *Till I ever work again.*
> *I'm not the man they think I am at home.*
> *Oh no no no, I'm J. Creeper man,*
> *J. Creeper man, hiding out, trying to escape*
> *my deeds.*

Something in me froze. Maybe it was my blood. Maybe it was all of me.

> *And I think it's gonna be a crazy, long time*
> *Till any stars play poker with me.*
> *I'm not the man they think I am at home.*
> *Oh no no no, I'm J. Creeper man,*
> *J. Creeper man, leching on all the girls at work.*

I wanted to turn it off, but I couldn't. It felt like someone threw a bucket of ice down my back and lit my stomach on fire. I only barely heard the yell from my sister's room. And I knew she was watching this too.

My show ain't the kind of place to turn your back.
My hands are everywhere.
If you turn me down, you'll lose your job.
And all this fuss, I don't understand.
I'm just a total pig five days a week.
J. Creeper man, J. Creeper man.

I heard my mom's footsteps as she ran to Kate's room. Voices. Kate saying something about Daddy and my mom telling her to turn it off.

Then the footsteps were heading to me and my closet room.

"Rodney?" said my mom. "Are you watchin—Oh no."

I'm not the man they think I am at home.
Oh no no no, I'm J. Creeper man,
Creeper man, maybe going to jail.

My mom reached out like she was going to take away my phone, but I held up my hand.

"No," I said. "Leave it."

Van kept singing, repeating the last lines, strumming his guitar, Ned and Blister keeping a beat on their drums. Then Van spoke into the camera again.

"I can't believe I had that guy on as a guest. My best girl Kylie worked for him. She said he was a creepy old boner king, but I thought she was just being a psycho. Sorry, Kylie. I should have believed you."

Behind him, Ned and Blister looked very serious, which didn't really suit their faces.

"Hey, J. Crederman, if you're listening, you are no longer welcome in the Johnsonverse. You're not lucky, dude. You're gross. You should apologize to Missy Stephenson and all your fans. Man, I can't believe I was one. I thought you were an OG. You let us down. Have some respect for the ladies, man."

I turned off YouTube. I could hear the blood sloshing around inside of me and hoped I wasn't going to get a clot in my superior vena.

J. Crederman. Jeremy Crederman. My dad.

I sort of heard my sister crying in her room, and I could feel my mom standing over me, and I could also feel her not knowing what to say.

Yup. Van Johnson sang about my dad, and when I turned it off, the video feed was showing two hundred thousand views. If my life wasn't ruined before, it is now.

Maybe talk later. But probably not.

Rodney

9

Hey, Larry,

Sorry about getting so upset about the Van Johnson thing. I mean, if you ever read this, you'll probably think I was overreacting and you'll be right. I guess I was just in shock. It was hard to believe Van Johnson did a whole song about my dad and also that he got it so wrong. My sister agrees with your mom that Van's an immature idiot, but Kate watches him too, because everyone does.

My mom made me and Kate meet her in the living room for a family meeting. Oh joy. I already hate family meetings due to how bad the last one was. We need another name for them. Life ruiner talks? Terrible news conversations?

"Rodney, Kate, I know that was painful to see, but the internet is not real life. It's not where we go to learn the truth about things," said my mom, which was funny because she goes on the internet every ten minutes to look up stuff about makeup and clothes and meditation and exercise.

But I've noticed she's not on there talking to her friends from back home either. I guess we have that in common.

Kate and my mom were on the only couch and I was in the only soft chair in the living room. None of it was very comfortable, probably because Mom's cousin Maria is so into exercise and being adventurous that she never bothered to get nice furniture that is good for relaxing on. She probably just uses the old couch to hold her climbing ropes and the easy chair for doing stretches or something. Maria looks like my mom, but also like everyone else around here: skinny and dusty and happy. Her girlfriend is from Germany and, in the pictures they have all around the house, she also looks dusty and happy, but she's twice as big as Maria, which is funny.

I looked at the big framed photo over the couch, where my mom sat rubbing Kate's back. It was a picture of Stony Butte taken from the top of the butte, and it was pretty impressive, with the pink-and-orange skies and dark-blue mountains way in the distance. The town itself was this little checkerboard below. It was nothing. It didn't matter. I thought about that while my mom tried to tell us that the Van Johnson thing wasn't a big deal. Ha.

Ha. Ha.

I was trying not to freak out. I thought about how you almost always stay cool in tense situations. Be like Larry, I told myself. It worked for a little while. But it was hard because Van Johnson's most popular videos, usually his songs, get watched by twenty or thirty million people. THIRTY. MILLION. PEOPLE. Listening to a song. About my dad. A song filled with lies.

"Can we sue him?" I asked.

"Who?" said my mom.

Kate looked at me like the chair just said something.

"Van Johnson. For telling lies."

My mom rubbed the knees of her exercise tights. She'd been working out in the living room when the video came on. The tights had cheetahs all over them.

"I think it's best just to let it go," she said. "Your father has, ah, shown poor judgment."

"He's been a pig!" said Kate.

I thought about my dad saying there had been some misunderstandings. I thought about how huggy he is. I think it's because of him being from England, which is practically in Europe, where everyone kisses everyone and hugs a lot. Dad said that some people are extremely sensitive and politically correct now, and I believe him, even though I'm not sure what politically correct means. I think it means that you get offended at the slightest thing. My dad says it's one of the worst things you can be. Which makes no sense, since Van Johnson's main thing is offending people.

My dad would never act like a creep with women at work. He's married to my mom, who wears cheetah tights and is very pretty. Everyone likes him and he's very funny and most of our friends wish they had a dad as cool as mine. Except maybe Johan, because it's even more cool to have a dad who is the lead singer in a band like 52 Pickup. Obviously, Johan's dad has a lot of tattoos and is really rich. But Johan is just like the rest of us. Just because his dad is a rock star doesn't make Johan a rock star. Johan is not as cool as his dad just like I'm not as cool as my dad.

I kept thinking about some of the sayings and quotes we learned at Circle Square to help our self-esteem. There was that one our teacher told us that was supposed to be from the Buddha? It was something like "Don't believe anything, no matter where you read it or who said it, not even if I have said it, unless it agrees with your own reason and your own common sense."

Then our teacher told us that the Buddha didn't really say that, and she explained about bad translations and misinformation, and we talked about how just because we find a quote on the internet doesn't mean we should believe it. She also said that the world was more complex than we imagine.

Overall, it was a pretty confusing talk that didn't do anything for my self-esteem. But I wish Buddha did say that quote because my common sense tells me that my dad didn't deserve that song.

"Look, kids," said my mom. "I know this must feel awful. It certainly does to me. But things won't always be like this. Your father has to deal with his own decisions."

"Are you guys getting divorced?" I asked.

My mom stared at me. I could see how hard she was trying to seem like everything was okay, even though it wasn't. "Rodney, I can't answer that."

I felt like someone cut the bottom out of my stomach and let my heart fall out.

"It's too soon to discuss what the future might bring," said my mom. "I just don't want you to worry." Ha. Ha, ha. Good one, Mom!

I hoped that meant she wasn't going to leave my dad. Because then we would have to live here forever, staring at stone butts in the sky.

"Thank god you registered us under your last name," said my sister. "Or there's no way I'd be going back to school."

She was right. Even if the song was wrong, I didn't want to be connected to it.

"People will forget," said my mom. "And we will adjust. We will keep adjusting. Humans are infinitely adaptable. Things will get better."

I didn't think I was infinitely adaptable. I was at my limit, adaptation-wise. I had a lot of questions. When would things get fixed? When would Missy Stephenson apologize? Why did Van Johnson talk about his friend Kylie? I didn't remember anyone on the crew with that name. It was all lies. I was going to say something, but my mom was sort of pale and sad, and Kate looked like an angry stick person, so I didn't. I would ask my dad next time we went to visit him. Maybe I would write Missy Stephenson a letter!

"Okay," I said. "It's fine."

"You're delusional," said my sister. "We are in hell and Daddy put us here."

So that's it for me, I guess.

Rodney

10

Hey, Larry,

I wonder how things are going at Circle Square? Are Tammy and Phil still trying to be co-class presidents because they can't be apart for ten seconds? Their parents must worry they're going to be the youngest people to ever get married in Vegas, which is, as you know, pretty young. To be honest, I wonder why I'm still writing this. Like I said, I'm never sending it. I guess talking to you is a habit, and even though all the talk is one-way, it still makes me feel better. Or something like that.

Here's the latest from Stony Butt if you're reading this, Stony Butte if my mom ever sees it. Ha.

After the Van Johnson video I was back to dreading school, even though no one knew my last name. I was fully in the yellow feeling zone when I walked in today. You might have forgotten our feelings colors since you were always in touch with how you feel. A refresher: Yellow zone is when you're afraid or upset. Red zone is angry and maybe even having a tantrum. Blue zone is when you're sad, sick, or bored. Green zone is happy and chill. Before we moved here, I thought I was comfortable with all the zones. What's that called? Emotionally regulated or something? Well, I'm not anymore. When a person gets stuck going from yellow to red to blue and back to yellow, it gets tiring. You never want to see yellow or red or blue ever again. You miss green!

When I opened the front doors of Stony Butte Elementary, I was so yellow I was like a nuclear banana. But I also tried to use the rules. Rule #3: Never Show an Unlucky Hand, #7: Don't Chase a Losing Streak, and #8: If Your Cards Keep Coming Up Bad, Change the Deck. But it was hard, because the rules are for poker and this wasn't poker.

I was afraid to even look at other people in case . . . well, in case they watched the video and somehow knew that J. Crederman was my dad. Thinking about how unfair it all was gave me a flash of red, but then I went back to yellow.

No one looked at me or noticed me, and I put my stuff in my locker and went to homeroom to wait for Mrs. Russo, our homeroom teacher. She is not Circle Square material, at all. It seems like she's just waiting for class to be over so she can go back to sleep. She's not mean or anything. She just seems extremely tired of being a teacher. She sighs about eight hundred times a class. It's actually sort of relaxing. She talks in this very soft, sleepy voice that makes it hard to stay awake. Lots of kids in my class sleep during homeroom, and I think that's how she wants it.

Dave waved me over, so I sat next to him.

He showed me the score he got on *Villainous* last night. It's this new game that everyone here is playing. Every character is a villain, such as a pirate or a demon or a serial killer, and they battle each other.

No one looked at me funny or said anything about Van Johnson, and I remembered that the internet isn't real life and Van Johnson is just some guy who makes videos in his basement. Of course he wasn't going to ruin my real life in the world.

My mood turned green for the first time since I saw the video. Sweet, sweet green!

I went to math and then language arts and we got tests back and both teachers gave me this look, like they were impressed. Mr. Woo, who is our language arts teacher, said, "Impressive work, Rodney," when he handed mine back. That was great because he's young and looks sort of like a poet who is also a rapper, if you know what I mean. He's got an earring and tattoos on one arm and he wears nice sneakers and he cares about language arts and students. Unlike Mrs. Russo, Mr. Woo is totally Circle Square material.

I was hanging out at lunch with Dave and Rigmor under the overhang between the buildings. My lunch was tasty, and I was still in a solid green zone situation.

My mom was right. It was all going to blow over.

Then Macii, who missed the morning because she had to go to the dentist, showed up.

She makes me nervous even though she speaks very, very quietly. There's just something about how she looks at me and how she talks about other people. She wraps her meanness in nice-girl wrapping paper, if you get my drift. Sort of like Breonnie Pickle at Circle Square. She smiles, and her voice is so soft that it takes a while to notice how much her words hurt.

When she came outside, she didn't say hi. I was showing Dave how to do this wooden 3-D puzzle thing that he got for his birthday. It's pretty hard, but I'm good at puzzles. I didn't pay attention to Macii. She went right over to Rigmor and started whispering. As usual.

But something in the air changed. It went a little yellow.

"What are you guys whispering about?" asked Dave.

I looked up.

Rigmor and Macii were staring. At me.

"What?" I said.

"What's your last name?" asked Macii, in her mean little voice.

I cleared my throat. "Garzi," I said.

"Really?" said Macii, in an extra softly mean voice. "Is that your *only* last name?"

I felt my eyes start to blink. I put the wood puzzle on the bench. Now they were all staring at me.

"Yes," I said.

"Really?" said Macii. She was so sweet, I felt like I might get sick.

"Stop saying that," said Rigmor, who actually *is* nice, and who has a proper voice that doesn't sound like it's coming out of a squirrel made of sugar.

Macii held up her phone. "So your last name isn't Crederman? And Jeremy Crederman the poker player *isn't* your dad?"

What's yellower than yellow? The sun? Death? That's the shade of yellow I was.

Was I supposed to lie?

But I didn't get a chance to say anything.

Macii turned her phone around and looked at something on the screen. "And this isn't you standing with J. Crederman on the red carpet here for the High Stakes Championship? Like, last year?"

Getting to be my dad's plus-one for the High Stakes award ceremony was the highlight of my whole life. Remember when we went shopping for my suit? And how my dad got you a suit too, just in case your mom won in the producer category? How was it possible that Macii could take one of my best memories and turn it into one of my worst?

"It says here that J. Crederman brought his son, *Rodney* Crederman, as his escort."

"How did you—?" I said.

"When I heard Van's song last night, I did some research. I always try to find out about people who do disgusting things. I found an article that said J. Crederman's family moved to Arizona. So I looked for pictures of him and his kids and there. You. Were. I have to say, I'm not surprised. I always had a weird feeling about you."

She smiled but not nicely.

I could tell that Rigmor and Dave didn't know what to say.

"So Rodney Creeperman," said Macii. "You've been lying to us."

"Macii," said Rigmor. But then she didn't say anything else.

"No, I haven't," I said. Except for changing my last name and never talking about my dad or what we were doing in Stony Butt, I didn't lie. I can't remember what that's called, but it's not lying, exactly.

"I personally am very uncomfortable with this," said Macii, sounding like she was giving a speech to the principal. "It's very deceptitious of you."

That's the other thing about Macii. She likes to use big words but doesn't know very many, so she just mangles them even worse than I do. I bet she's not getting any special compliments from Mr. Woo.

The buzzer rang and everyone got up, like we were being ordered by a remote control. We packed up our lunch stuff and went to our next classes, and I wondered if I was in the middle of a nightmare, one of those ones that just gets worse and worse.

So that's it for now. Hope you are good.

Rodney

11

Hey, Larry,

Okay, just one more update. Just in case you wondered what happened after the thing with Macii.

As soon as history was over, I practically ran out of class. I tried not to look at anyone so I wouldn't have to see if they were looking at me.

I hoped Macii wouldn't tell everyone about my dad, but I knew she probably would. I just wanted to get out of there. And obviously I wasn't going to go with Rigmor to see her brother at the comics store.

I headed for the side door. I wanted to avoid the front of the school in case Macii was out there, whispering away at everyone, showing them the picture of me and my dad.

I know Circle Square has a no bullying policy, but remember when that one girl got bullied because the newspapers found out her mom, who was a big-deal politician, was hiring undocumented workers and not paying them properly? No one was mean to her, but we all kind of stayed away from her after that. Even the teachers seemed a little uncomfortable with her because Circle Square believes in human rights and not taking advantage of other people.

Well, I was just hoping that's how things would go for me. People would ignore me and I could ignore them back.

I headed across the field so I could take a side street home. I was one of the first outside, so I figured I could get away without people seeing me.

I thought I was clear when I heard a voice behind me.

"Hey! Rodney!"

I almost kept going.

"RODNEY!" came the voice again.

It is impolite to ignore people, so I looked back.

It was Rigmor. She was running after me in her bright-green chucks, long white hair streaming behind her like a ribbon.

"Wait up," she said, even though I'd already stopped to wait for her.

"Aren't we going to my brother's store?" she said.

I looked at my shoes. They were also green. I never used to be a shoe looker. I used to look people in the eyes. That's gone too.

"I don't know," I said.

I took a chance and looked at her.

Her eyes are dark blue, and her eyebrows are much darker than her pale hair. Rigmor isn't just nice. She is extremely pretty. Not that I wanted to notice, especially right then. I felt like a terrible person for noticing.

"Yes, dummy. We made a plan. I told my brother we were coming."

I didn't know whether I should bring up the thing with Macii or the thing with my dad. If I did, maybe Rigmor would change her mind. And I didn't want that. My emotions felt tired out. Like someone smeared all of the colors together and now I just felt muddy.

"Come on," she said.

So basically, it was a top-five worst day, but it was also not completely terrible. I've got to go have a pot pie. I'll finish this after dinner, even though I said this was the last thing I'd say about this today. I wish I could send you a Perfect Pie. They would blow your mind.

Take care,

Rodney

12

Hey, Lar,

I'm back. Again! I'll just finish telling you about what happened because it was pretty interesting—at least, I think so.

Cruel Comix was small, but it had everything we love. Independent comics and lots of manga, older editions and collections. It also had good board games, new and used, and some toys. I'm not a comic book expert. You know way more than I do, but I think even you would be impressed.

Rigmor's brother, Nils, was helping a customer when we came in. Nils looks like Rigmor, but he's older, maybe nineteen or twenty, and his white hair is shorter, and he has glasses and a thin neck, and he looks like he should manage a comic-book store.

There were a few customers in the store—older guys, mostly, some with beards and some wearing all black clothes. Finally, some people in Stony Butte who didn't look like they mountain biked and ran and skydived every single day. These guys looked like they knew their way around a game console, which I found relaxing.

Nils didn't say anything to us until his customers left and it was just the three of us in the little store, which was crammed full of stuff, but in a good way.

"Rigs," he said. "How was your day?"

"My day was fine. His day, not so much," she said, pointing at me.

I felt my eyes bug out. What was she doing?

"Oh yeah?" said Nils. "What happened?" Nils is very pale, and he looks like he makes a point of staying up late.

"Some stuff at school," said Rigmor. "It reminded me of you."

I didn't like where the conversation was going even though I didn't completely understand what she was talking about.

"Oh, sorry," Rigmor said, noticing my face. "I forgot to introduce you. Rodney, this is my brother, Nils. Nils, Rodney."

Nils held his long, skinny hand out for me to shake across the counter.

"So what's going on? With the bad day? Or maybe you don't want to talk about it?" said Nils. "I can just give you a tour of the store."

"His dad is J. Crederman," said Rigmor.

WHAT WAS SHE TRYING TO DO TO ME?

I stared at her. Maybe this was all some big setup and she was just as mean as Macii. I should have gone straight home.

"Oh." Nils' voice was all worried, like she just told him I was not toilet trained or something.

"And, of course, Macii had to tell everyone. Rodney just moved here."

"I see," said Nils. He adjusted his glasses, which were big and a little smudged.

I wanted to leave, but I was stuck from all my politeness training. I decided when I got out of the store, I would leave town. Go and live . . . somewhere else. Not in Vegas, obviously. Not here because it sucked and because my cover story was gone. I could go to . . . When I couldn't think of a single place to go, I got this feeling in my chest. Don't cry, I told myself. Not here. Not in front of Rigmor and Nils and all the superheroes.

But I sure wanted to cry. I would only admit that to you because I know you'd understand.

"Your dad is a genius," said Nils. "I've sold so many copies of *Get Lucky*. And I love his shows. What's happening to him is a disgrace."

My head snapped up.

"That's right. This whole thing where people get their lives ruined for nothing has gone too far. I read about it. Your dad says he didn't do anything wrong. And I know from experience that's probably true. Missy Stephenson and those other ones are just trying to ruin him."

I couldn't believe it. He was saying what I thought! Finally! Someone who got it.

I looked from Rigmor to Nils.

"Nils got accused of touching a girl when he was in eleventh grade. At a dance at the high school. She said he

93

grabbed her and worse stuff too. They were going to throw him out of school. Everyone said he was dangerous."

Nils nodded. His pale face had gone pink and there were red blotches on his neck.

"The only reason my life wasn't ruined was because there was a camera in the hallway where she said it happened," he said.

Rigmor's face was serious. She looked way older than any other sixth grader I know.

"The girl finally told the truth," said Rigmor. "She told them she said what she said because he asked another girl to the dance and that made her jealous. Nils had to talk to counselors and he even had to get interviewed by the police."

"People thought I was a criminal," said Nils. His voice was all hoarse and he sounded like he was going to be upset about what happened for the rest of his life. "There are still people in this town who think I've got a problem. There are still girls who avoid me."

"That's just 'cause of the comics," said Rigmor. She was holding a doll of Princess Leia in a bikini, busting the chain Jabba the Hutt put on her. "I think they avoid you because you game all the time and read comics. This isn't Brooklyn, you know."

"Darn straight it's not. And anyway, what do you know about Brooklyn?" said Nils. He smiled at her.

"I know you want to move there one day," said Rigmor.

Nils turned to me. "Look, ignore what people say about your dad. All this stuff about how everyone has to believe women or girls or whatever? Take it from me: don't."

"Until there's proof," said Rigmor. She put Princess Leia back on the shelf, next to the box containing Jabba the Hutt. Then she changed her mind and put Leia next to Skywalker.

So that's it. I still can't believe someone is on my side here. Or my dad's side, I guess.

Maybe I'll send you a game invite soon. You could try out *Villainous* with me and Dave and Rigmor. Not Macii. I'm never playing with her again.

Okay, so that's definitely all that happened today.

Take care,

Rodney

13

Hey, Lar,

I thought I'd get to spend homeroom writing to you about how boring last weekend was, but then today happened, and it was the opposite of boring. It was also the opposite of good.

You probably saw some of this, but I thought you might like to hear about it from me.

This morning, Monday, my mom dropped my sister at the high school. No one at her school knew about our dad, so I felt a bit jealous.

Then we drove the two blocks to my school. I was pretty nervous but at least I'd be able to count on Rigmor to be friendly.

We pulled into the drop-off area and I got out of the car. Before I knew what was happening, a bunch of people came rushing over and surrounded me, taking photos and trying to look in the car so they could take my mom's picture and ask her questions. I didn't know what to do, and when I looked at my mom, I could tell she didn't know what to do either. That was rough. She looked like a kid. I wanted to get back in the car, but maybe the reason they were here was because they found out about me and didn't know about my mom yet, so I just pretended the photographers and the grown-ups yelling questions at me weren't there. I tried to be like one of those people you see on TV when they go into court and ignore all the reporters who are trying to ask them questions.

I tried to walk into the school and all around me people were yelling: Rodney. Rodney? Rodney! How does it feel, Rodney? Tell us about your dad, Rodney.

A lady with shiny black hair and a lot of makeup got so close to me that I could smell her perfume and her breath that reeked like coffee and mints. "Rodney? It's Rodney, right?" she said in an English accent. She started following me and so did a guy with a big video camera. I thought they were going to come right in the school with me.

"Do you have anything to say, Rodney?"

"What has your father said about his crimes?"

"Is he worried about so many women pressing charges?"

"Is it true he's tried to apologize to Missy Stephenson?"

"When's the last time you saw your father? How's he doing?"

"What about the allegations from employees?"

The lady and her cameraman got ahead of me so they were blocking the way. I turned and ran right into a wall of people. I couldn't see my mom anymore, or our car. I turned around again just in time to see someone knock the shiny lady and the camera guy and a bunch of other people out of the way.

It was Chum! I mean, Fisherman! He was practically as big as the cameraman and he said "scram" or some other small-town thing that means get lost. Then he called them "stupid lamestream media." Then he picked me up again and *carried* me into the school. My own dad hasn't carried me as much as Fisherman has in the last few weeks. It's probably not too manly to mention it, but it is interesting.

This time, he didn't run out the other end of the school with me and try to head-slam me into the soccer net at the far end of the field. He put me down outside the nurse's office, like he wasn't sure I could stand on my own. I wasn't so sure about that either because my knees started to shake.

I just kind of wobbled there for a while.

"Okay, Rod?" he asked. I don't love the name Rod, but it's better than his nickname, so I didn't correct him.

I nodded.

"Fake media are scum," he said. "All liars."

There was a time when my dad and I would have laughed our faces off if we heard something like that. My dad told me that only people who have no media literacy think all stories that they don't agree with are fake news. Media literacy means that you understand about newspapers and TV shows and understand which ones tell true stories using proper journalism and which ones are fake. But times were different. Maybe *all* those people out there waiting for me and my mom *were* fake news.

"Is my mom okay?" I asked. I couldn't believe I'd just left her there.

"She's okay. When she saw I had you, she drove away," said Fisherman. Fisherman bent down and got really close to my face. His breath smelled like cereal. I think in future I would like not to smell anyone's breath. I might be getting a phobia about it.

"Don't let it get you down, man," he said.

And then he stomped off down the hall to his classroom. I couldn't quite believe what just happened. We got attacked by journalists and my mom just left? I guess I was happy she got away, but what the heck?

I waited until I felt steadier on my feet and then went into the bathroom to fix myself up after Fisherman tackle-saved me. Also, to be honest, I was worried I might start crying or something.

The guys in the bathroom stopped talking when I walked in.

I felt dumb with them all staring at me, so I just took a piece of paper towel and left. They all started talking again when I left.

Same thing in class. Everyone shut up as soon as I walked in, including Dave and Rigmor, who were in the same class. Rigmor waved, but it was a small wave.

I didn't say hello to anyone or wave back. I'm not sure why not.

After I sat down, people started whispering again. Because she's so tired, Mrs. Russo is always late.

While we waited, Lallie, the girl with the long blonde braids wrapped around her head who didn't like my T-shirt on the first day, spoke up loud enough for the whole class to hear. Everyone stopped talking.

"I don't feel safe with him here."

At first, I didn't even realize she was talking about me. She is always feeling very uncomfortable or unsafe about one thing or another.

"Not only is his father a predator, I think he looks at me funny too. My mom says that unclean thoughts and acts run in families."

I stopped breathing.

Unclean thoughts and acts. That sounded terrible. Like something a person needed to be ashamed of. Also, "predator" didn't seem good.

"Plus, the media circus," said Lallie, and the way she said it I could tell she just learned those words. "It's harming my educational opportunities. I felt unsafe when I had to walk through all those reporters on the way into school today. A few of those reporters asked me for an interview."

Lallie's skin is almost the same yellowish color as her hair and she has a pinched-up little face. Talking about how dangerous I was made her look happier than I'd ever seen her. She and Macii should be best friends, but they can't stand each other. I don't blame them. I'm not crazy about them either.

"I said no, because I had to go to class. But I may talk to them later. I might give them an exclusive."

I felt my mouth fall open. What would Lallie talk to them about? Braid crowns? I'd never talked to her before, except on the first day about our pool. I definitely never looked at her in any bad way, other than to wonder how long her hair was that it could wrap around her head so many times.

101

A voice came from the corner of the room. It was Ben. I hadn't even noticed him come in. He has this way of being sort of invisible in class.

"Why don't you just mind your own business, Lallie?"

Everyone stared, mouths open. Ben never talks in class. Lallie's mouth snapped shut and she glared at him.

"Why don't you shut up, you illegal."

People all over class made a gasping noise like they just got hit in the back at the same time.

"Maybe I should get my mom to call immigration on you," she continued, looking at Ben and a bunch of kids in the back row.

"Go ahead," said Ben. "My dad has work papers."

"Not for long," said Lallie.

"You don't have to win the nastiest person prize every day, Lallie," said Rigmor. Her pale face was all splotchy like Nils's had been when he told me what happened to him.

Lallie shut up. Rigmor is like Ben. She doesn't talk much, but when she does people listen.

And after that, people stopped whispering and staring at me and instead went sort of back to normal. The teacher still hadn't shown up. Maybe she fell asleep in the staff room.

Not for me, though. Nothing felt normal to me.

Dave was waiting for me outside after math was over, right before lunch.

"The principal and school security made the reporters leave," he said.

"Oh," I said.

"I stayed out there and watched. After Chum picked you up."

"Okay," I said.

"Coming to the benches for lunch?"

I didn't answer.

"Rodney?" asked Dave. "You okay?"

"Yeah," I said, because I couldn't think what else to say.

We were almost at the hallway when Dave stopped and looked at me. "Do you want to talk about what happened? Is it true about your dad? And that song Van Johnson did. Is that real?"

I realized right then that I'd been thinking that if I just ignored it, everything would go away. I thought about trying to use my dad's Rules to Live a Lucky Life. But they weren't going to fix this. Because I wasn't lucky. Neither was my dad, at least not right now. What if my dad couldn't prove the people who were accusing him were lying?

"I gotta go," I said and walked away from Dave and away from Stony Butte Elementary. I went out the side door again, just in case the reporters were still hanging around the front. I walked across the playing field, then headed for home on a strange street. I found myself wishing Ben would show up on his bike. I bet he wouldn't have asked me any questions. He would just ask me if I wanted to do some dangerous activity. That would have been okay with me, because I would have preferred to jump into the gorge again than talk.

When I got home, the Range Rover was in the driveway. I let myself in and found my mom sitting at the kitchen table. She jumped to her feet and came over and hugged me.

"Oh, honey," she said. "I'm so sorry I left you there. I thought it would be safest for you. I thought they'd follow me and I could get them . . . away from you. But they didn't follow. I've been on the phone with the school to make sure you were okay, but they couldn't find you."

"Is Kate here?" I asked.

"No," she said. My mom's hair, which had been up in this kind of knot-thing, had come loose. Her eyes were red and her face was tight. She was in her work clothes, even though I don't think she went to work.

I didn't want to say any more, so I just went into my closet. So that's it. And you know what, Larry. I'm sorry that you aren't speaking to me, but maybe now I'm not speaking to you either.

Rodney

14

Hey, Larry,

Who am I kidding? Of course I'm speaking to you, or at
least writing to you, even if you don't know it. Who else
am I going to talk to? Ha. Anyway, I have some news that
will surprise you. I am a juvenile delinquent now! So is
Kate! Our whole family has gone outlaw.

Background: Kate didn't come home after school after
the reporters tracked us down. My mom nearly lost her
mind. Off to the side note: my mom tried to call the principal from Kate's school, but the teachers here don't give
out their personal numbers like they do at Circle Square.

Luckily, Kate called at 6:00 p.m. and told us that she
had gone to the city and was staying with either Cavendish
or Lavender. I'm not sure which.

Anyway, Kate was at least safe. But by the time she
called, my mom had already called the police. They told
her they couldn't search for someone until she'd been gone
for more than a few hours. They also asked if anything

had happened to upset Kate recently. When they asked that, my mom hung up on them.

When Kate finally called to tell us where she was, my mom told her all the bad things that happen to people who run away. I tuned out. I was eating a Mrs. Perfect turkey pot pie, which tastes almost exactly like the Mrs. Perfect chicken pot pie, but more turkey-ish. My mom looked at me a few times, like she was wondering how I could eat pot pie at such a time, but she doesn't understand pot pie or peas or being almost twelve. I might be having a growth spurt from all the stress. My stomach seems to be having one. It seems important to mention that the turkey pot pie had just as many peas as the chicken pot pie.

My sister asked to talk to me, but I said I was too busy eating. Which was true. I knew Kate would text me later and I planned to ignore her.

Later that night my mom's boss called. I know because my mom came into my closet room after she talked to her and said she was going back to work the next day. She said her new boss was being very understanding about everything.

"Are you still going to teach your Pilates classes?" I asked.

"I think so," she said. "Everyone needs more core strength."

"What if no one comes because of . . . ?"

"The thing with your father?" she finished. "Then I'll do Pilates by myself."

But I knew people would show up. People would be curious about what kind of person would marry

J. Crederman. That made me sad. Back in Vegas, everyone went to my mom's classes because she was a great teacher and very fit.

Anyway, the next morning, I told my mom I wasn't going to school.

"Rodney, you have to," said my mom. "It's the rule."

"Not for Kate."

"It's the rule for Kate too. She's just breaking it."

"Sorry," I said. "I'm just not up to it."

"I can't let you stay home alone. I have to go to work. They already let me stay home yesterday. I can't strain Nancy's patience anymore."

"Maybe we should hire someone to homeschool me. A nanny who is also a teacher."

My mom stared at me. She looked like herself again. All shiny and neat and ready to do something with insurance. That was nice to see.

"We no longer have the budget for a nanny. Or even a babysitter. We definitely can't afford a nanny-teacher, if there's such a thing."

"There is. They're called governesses. I've read about them. Some kids at Circle Square had one, I think."

"I'm the only nanny in this house and I work in insurance now."

I like that my mom isn't embarrassed that she used to be a nanny fitness instructor. My half sister and her mom are mean about it, but they're mean about everything.

"Mom. I'm not going," I said.

"I can't stay home or we'll go broke."

"I'll stay inside. I won't get in trouble."

I could tell she didn't know what to do or say.

"I'm not dumb. You can leave me alone for a few hours."

She leaned against the counter in the little kitchen. I shouldn't have confused her by getting dressed like I was going to school. I should have stayed in bed so it was clear.

"Rodney, do you want to talk about your dad? About what happened?"

"No," I said. "I know what happened and I don't want to talk about it right now. If you try, I'll . . ."

She waited.

"Run away," I said. "Or join a gang."

I could tell she didn't believe me. I didn't believe me either.

"A water polo gang," I said, so she knew I wasn't serious.

"You can't put off going back to school forever."

That's where she was wrong. I am very good at putting things off.

"We're going to see your dad this weekend," she said. "And I think we need to clear the air. Deal with reality."

I shrugged. I was taking a mentally healthy day. That's what my dad used to call it when he stayed home from work. There were only a few. One time he taught me how to play blackjack until Mom reminded him of the no cards at home rule. It was fun, just me and him doing something together.

After trying to make me go to school for a little while longer, my mom gave up. She went to work and left me at home by myself, which is probably illegal.

I tried to play games, but no one was online, probably

because they were in school. I thought about messaging you, but then remembered that we aren't speaking.

I watched YouTube videos on the laptop for a while, but my mom has the censorship level cranked up so far, I might as well be five.

Then I had a snack.

By the time it was 10:00 a.m. I was really bored. My mom called and asked how I was.

"Fine," I said. "Doing homework."

Which wasn't a total lie. I put the books on the kitchen table in a way that looked homework-y in case she came home for lunch. I totally *planned* to do homework at some point in the future, but not right now.

At 10:20 a.m. someone knocked on the door.

For the first time, I felt nervous. This was basically the first time I'd been left home alone without an adult around. If there was a criminal murderer at the door, the little house didn't even have an alarm or a housekeeper to call the police or anything.

Then the doorbell rang.

Maybe it was a reporter. I would rather be at school than talk to one of them.

I punched 9-1-1 into my phone and held my finger right over the Call button. The door doesn't even have a peephole!

"Hello?" I said, and I made my voice all low and mature and not like the voice of someone who would be easy to kill.

"You home?"

It was not a smart question. Obviously, whoever was

answering the door was home. Obviously, whoever was at the door was not a genius.

"Who's asking?" I said, and I felt like I was in one of those old movies my dad watches about tough guys who never say more than three words, all of them rude.

"It's Ben. Chum's here too."

"Don't call me Chum," I heard another voice say.

"What are you guys doing here?" I asked. For some reason, I felt nervous to have them here even though they are sort of friends.

"You're not at school," said Ben.

"Neither are you," I said.

"We got an idea." Fisherman's voice. Now I was really scared. Fisherman didn't seem like an ideas man to me.

"You going to let us in?" asked Ben.

I stood right next to the locked door with them on the other side. The little house felt safe, which was strange because I don't even like it that much and would rather be back in our old house in my old life. In how things used to be.

But then I remembered that nowhere was safe and that our old life was gone. I opened the door.

Ben stood in the doorway. He was exactly half as wide as Fisherman.

"Why aren't you guys in school?" I asked.

"Needed a day off," said Ben, like every second day wasn't a day off for him thanks to his sports.

"I'm here 'cause there's a test," said Fisherman. "In English. No thank you."

They didn't ask me why I wasn't in school. I suppose they knew.

110

I wondered why Ben and his dad and brothers didn't just go back to Canada. I would go to Canada if someone asked me. But not the cold part. Does Canada have warm parts? I should find out. I kept my questions to myself.

"You want to come in?" I asked, even though I really didn't want them to. I'd have been embarrassed for anyone from back home to see how small and old this house is. But I'd seen where Ben lives, and something told me that Fisherman's house isn't that great either. My mom would have a freak if I had people over while she was away.

"Nah," said Fisherman. "We're going to the ranch."

"His uncle has a ranch," said Ben. "It's called Rancho Socorro."

"Yeah," said Fisherman. "My aunt and uncle are the managers. They're trailering a horse to Albuquerque and will be gone all day."

"A horse?" I said.

"I brought a bike for you. Let's go," said Ben.

Ten minutes later we were riding bikes in a direction I'd never gone, and it wasn't hot and it wasn't cold and the road was straight and flat and the sky ahead was almost the same shade of red as the sand and I was green as a Vegas golf course.

I've got to stop now so I can do more illegal stuff. J.K. It's dinnertime and my Mrs. Perfect is waiting.

Yours delinquently,

Rodney

15

Hey, Lar,

I'm back. Now where was I? Oh, right. The Ranch.

It looked like nothing because it looked the same as everything else.

Fisherman stopped his bike, which was almost twice the size of the mountain bikes Ben and I rode and still looked like he'd stolen it from a four-year-old.

"Here it is," he said.

I looked around for a log house, horses and cowboys and cows, but there was only a double-wide trailer, empty pens, and one longer fenced area that ran behind three old barns and alongside the road for a little way.

"Cool," said Ben, and I think he was actually serious. Rancho Socorro wasn't that cool.

"Where is everything?" I asked.

Fisherman didn't answer. He just sniffed and wiped his nose on the bottom of his shirt. I thought wiping your nose on your sleeve was extremely outlaw. I never even knew that the bottom of the shirt was an option.

"My uncle lets me use his gun sometimes. We do target practice over there," he said and pointed off behind the barn.

I felt my eyes bulge. Guns? Remember how I said when I first saw him that he might have weapons? I was right! Can you imagine what our teachers at Circle Square would say to hear we were near actual weapons? Or our parents? Your mom especially! So much for Disarm and Live Day, where we wrote letters to members of Congress.

I cleared my throat.

"Don't worry, I won't shoot you if you're against the Second Amendment," said Fisherman.

It was the first sign that Fisherman knew at least part of the Constitution. I was impressed, even though at Circle Square we learned it at the beginning of fourth grade.

"Anything to eat here?" asked Ben.

"That sounds great!" I said, sounding all high-pitched due to being afraid of guns and hoping Fisherman wouldn't be bringing one out. I was so nervous I almost wished I was in school getting called a predator instead of at Rancho Scare-o with no adult supervision. "I could go for a snack." It wasn't true. The gun talk ruined my appetite.

"I'm not supposed to go inside when my aunt and uncle aren't here," said Fisherman. "And I'm not allowed to touch the guns."

We were standing in a wide dirt area between the trailer and the barn. There was an old truck with a flat tire parked against the barn, and I could see a shiny orange tractor parked inside a shed.

"Your aunt and uncle live here?" I asked.

"Yeah. They manage the ranch. The owner is some rich guy from L.A. who never even visits. My uncle says the guy just likes telling people he has a ranch."

Just then a black-and-white dog that looked as old as rocks came out from behind the barn. Its knees didn't really bend, so it tilted from side to side with every step when it walked.

"Willy!" said Fisherman, sounding happier than I'd ever heard him sound before. "Hey, buddy."

He got down on one knee and scratched the old dog behind its ears. Its eyes were a little bit cloudy, and it seemed like it might be mostly blind, but it was happy to be with Fisherman.

"Willy's the best," said Fisherman. "I love him." Then he turned bright red and coughed, like he'd said something stupid or like we were going to make fun of him.

"Nice dog," I said, so he wouldn't feel bad.

Ben nodded.

"Yeah." Fisherman stopped petting Willy even though the danger of us laughing had passed. "What do you guys want to do?"

I was praying Ben didn't ask more about the guns. This was how accidents happened.

My armpits were sweating and I hoped the guys couldn't see. I even felt a little dizzy. Maybe I could say I was sick and go home. Or I could pretend to get a message from my mom and say she wanted me home. But I didn't want to wuss out in front of Fisherman and Ben.

"I'll show you guys some stunts," said Ben. "But are you sure we can't get a little snack first?"

For a second, Fisherman seemed like he was going to say no again, but he probably wanted Ben to think he was cool. He thought for a second and then said okay. Fisherman made us turn around so we wouldn't see when he got the key out of its hiding place. Ben peeked though.

"Wait here," said Fisherman, and he disappeared into the trailer.

"Have you ever been here before?" I asked Ben in a whisper while we waited for Fisherman to come back.

"Nah. I never even really hung out with him before. But we get along at school."

I nodded.

"You're bringing people together, man," said Ben. He was grinning.

His words made me feel good, which was a nice change from scared.

"You guys can come in now," said Fisherman from the top steps of a small wooden porch. We followed him inside the trailer. It was neat but old, and not the antique kind of old where everything is all wooden and expensive, but just old and not very fancy.

"It's big," I said, because I didn't know what else you were supposed to say. I definitely wouldn't be telling Fisherman's aunt and uncle about how we used to have an in-ground Olympic pool and a house with six bedrooms. They'd probably shoot me.

"Stay on the mat," said Fisherman. "I'll finish getting the stuff."

"Can I look in the fridge?" asked Ben.

Fisherman just held up a hand like he wanted us to be quiet. "I'll tell my aunt I got hungry," he muttered. "She probably won't say anything to my dad."

I thought about how my mom or our nanny would get us any snacks we wanted, whenever we wanted, as long as they didn't have sugar or preservatives in them.

Ben and I stood just inside the door, and I tried not to look around too much, because that would be rude.

Fisherman was taking things from the cupboard without even looking and stuffing them into his jacket and jean pockets. No picnic basket for him.

He came back toward us, practically running.

"Okay, let's go."

We all piled out of the trailer and I felt sick and excited, like we'd just robbed it.

He made us turn around again while he locked the door, and there was a dull thud on the little porch.

"Dang," he said. "I dropped the peaches."

Ben and I looked at each other.

"It's okay," said Fisherman, his face red. "They didn't break."

"What'd you get?" asked Ben.

Fisherman didn't answer. He led us into the first barn. It was two stories tall and had a loft. It smelled like dirt and animals, even though there were no animals in it, and there was hay all over the floor. The loft was filled with bales of hay too. If one of those fell on you, you'd be dead for sure. The whole place was deadly. Guns, illegal snacks, hay bales. Probably pitchforks and gopher holes too.

117

Fisherman pulled over an old wooden crate to use as a table and started unloading stuff from his pockets and jacket. A jar of peaches, four sticks of pepperoni, a loose handful of crackers (with gluten, I figured, which would be awesome). There was an apple and a few cubes of white sugar and three cucumbers.

"Arigatō, tomodachi," said Ben.

"Is that Spanish?" asked Fisherman.

"Japanese," said Ben, through a mouth full of cucumber.

"Are you Japanese?"

"My dad's Japanese Canadian."

"Oh. Can you speak Japanese?" asked Fisherman.

"All I can do is order sushi and say hello, please, and thank you," said Ben.

"My dad says all the foreigners are going to have to go home," Fisherman said.

Fisherman didn't seem like he was trying to be rude, even though he was being incredibly rude.

"This is home, sort of," said Ben. "I've been here since I was four."

Fisherman ate another cracker. It looked like a cornflake in his huge hands.

"Are you going to get deported?" I asked, and nearly choked on my cracker because I was surprised by my own words.

Ben sighed. "I don't know. My mom went back to Canada last year. She said she doesn't like it here. But if we leave, we probably won't be able to ever come back. Because we overstayed."

"Never?" I said.

"I don't think so," said Ben. "My dad says he needs to

be able to work in the U.S. But my mom gets lots of stunt work in Canada. I think he just likes it here."

"You must miss your mom," I said.

"Yeah." Ben's face didn't look so confident anymore.

"I went to Canada once," said Fisherman. "We went to a rodeo in Calgary. Back when my uncle did roping."

"Was it nice?" asked Ben. "Calgary, I mean."

"Pretty good rodeo," said Fisherman.

I felt bad for Ben and his family, but I was also glad I wasn't the only one who had problems.

"So you're going to teach us some stuff?" asked Fisherman. "Stunts and tricks like your mom and dad do?"

"My brothers too," said Ben. He looked around, like he was trying to get ideas. "We could jump off that loft into that hay," he said. "I'll show you how to roll so you don't get too hurt."

Too hurt. My heart dropped into my stomach. Great. My back killed me for days after I'd hit it on the cliff.

"Or we could use that lumber to build a couple of bike jumps we can gap," said Ben.

"Yeah," I said, even though I was also afraid of crashing on a bike. At least the bike jump wasn't going to be off the second story of a huge building, which is something trick riders like to do.

"As long as we put everything back," said Fisherman. "We're not really supposed to be here alone."

"Beware the Truancy Monster," said Ben.

"Truancy Monster?" I asked.

"Stony Butte has the biggest truancy officer you ever saw," said Fisherman.

"What's that?" I said.

They stared at me.

"He's like a cop who makes you go to school," said Ben.

"If you don't go, he'll take you to juvie jail," said Fisherman.

"You don't want that," said Ben. "That place is supposed to be bad news. He came over to our place once, but I just had to update my paperwork. I was riding in a Rock 'Em Energy Refresher video with my brothers so I was allowed to miss school."

Then we stopped talking and just ate. At first, I ate just to be polite, and then I ate because it was all really good, even if it was a weird mix of things. Maybe doing illegal and dangerous activities was good for the appetite.

The peaches were especially delicious, even though they were slimy, and we had to eat them with our hands and then wipe our hands on the hay (me and Ben) or our pants (Fisherman).

"My aunt cans," said Fisherman.

"My uncle bottles," I said, trying to be funny. But none of us got the joke exactly, because I guess I'm not good with ranch humor yet.

When we finished eating, we started building.

It was actually fun and a bit educational, Larry. I think you might have liked it. There's more, but I'm going to take a break. Maybe have a pot pie.

Arigatō!

Rodney the Wild

16

Hey, Lar,

I'm back! There's more!

We built two jumps using plywood and boards over hay bales that we could ride up and over. Ben hit the first jump and flew right over the second one. Fisherman hit the ramp and it collapsed. I hit the ramp and fell into the space between the jumps. I sacked myself so hard that I couldn't stand up for, like, ten minutes because I couldn't breathe. The guys thought that was hilarious.

I also slipped off the side of the ramp once and hurt my elbow and scraped all the skin off the side of my leg.

I fell coming off the side of the second jump another time because I was going so slow and bashed my other elbow.

It wasn't that fun from a getting-hurt perspective.

Ben kept moving the jumps further and further apart and then he got Fisherman to lay down in between them. That's when I took a break. I wandered over to look into the fenced pasture.

That's when I saw the horse.

He came trotting over. His coat was a reddish-gold color and he had a long dark mane and tail. His eyes were black and there was black on his nose and legs. I walked toward him and he made a horse noise that sounded like hello. I have to tell you, man, it was amazing.

Fisherman came over. He wasn't injured, so I guess Ben didn't land on him.

"That's Kingdom Come Lately. We call him King. He probably wants sugar. You can feed him if you want."

I looked at Fisherman, not quite getting what he meant.

"The sugar cubes I took from inside. They're for feeding to the horses. He's the only one who'll come to visit though. The rest of the herd aren't that social. My uncle says he's real quirky. Just don't go in the pen with him and you'll be fine."

"Hey, that's a nice horse," said Ben, pushing his bike over. He was the only one of us who wasn't covered in scratches and bruises.

I didn't want to leave the horse, but I also really wanted to feed him, so I ran back to the barn and got the cubes. I ran back out and slowed down when Kingdom's head went up. A person probably shouldn't run around horses.

"Hi," I said, and he made a snorting noise. Up close he was big and covered in dust but also somehow kind of shiny and he smelled very horsey, which is a surprisingly nice smell.

"Okay, I'm going to give you a sugar cube now, so don't bite off my fingers," I said, barely even noticing that I was talking out loud to a horse. I looked around to see Ben was practicing on the bike jumps again and Fisherman was saying something to him.

King arched his neck and sniffed my hand and I held out the sugar cube between two fingers. He took it from me and his lips were soft, and I could feel his whiskers brush against my hand.

"Not like that," said Fisherman. "Hold your hand flat."

I took a deep breath, put another sugar cube in my palm, and held my hand out, like I was asking for something. He took the piece of sugar just as gently as he had the first time.

He also let me pet his neck and I took a few sniffs of him. I never thought anything that wasn't a girl's perfume or fresh baking could smell so nice. I can't quite explain it, but being close to the horse made me feel better than I had since we'd got to Stony Butte. The horse made my insides feel calm.

I was so happy when he didn't walk away after he ate all the sugar cubes. He sniffed me and I sniffed him and I kept giving him pats. That probably sounds weird but it wasn't.

"You want to do the course once more before we take it down?" asked Fisherman.

I shook my head, still staring at King. "Do people ride him?" I asked.

"Not yet. He's still green. My uncle's real into that natural horsemanship stuff so he doesn't start 'em until they're a little older. I think King's broke to halter and he's been lunged, but nothing else. My uncle says he has a few quirks, so he's taking it real slow with him."

123

I had no idea what any of that meant.

"How old is he?"

I finally looked back at Fisherman, who shrugged.

"Maybe two and a half?"

I wanted to know everything about King, but it would have sounded like I was in love with him, which, if I'm being real, I guess I sort of was. Not that I'd say that to anyone but you because it sounds weird. Maybe I was more, like, in awe of him than in love.

"You sure you don't want to ride the course again?"

Something about being near the horse made it feel okay to say that I didn't want to.

"Before we go, we need to put everything away. If we leave a mess, I'll be working here for free for a year."

"You work here? Doing what?"

"I help with the horses. Fix fences. Make sure they all have water. Unload hay. Stuff like that."

"Can I help?" The words were out of my mouth before I could even think them properly.

"My uncle pays me, like, three dollars an hour," said Fisherman. "I only do it because my mom says I have to. And because sometimes he lets me shoot his guns after church."

"I don't need to get paid. And I don't want to shoot."

Fisherman stared at me like I just farted.

"Serious? No pay and you don't want to shoot?"

I nodded. "I wouldn't mind learning about ranching. And horses."

He gave a little laugh. "If you say so. I'll ask my uncle."

"I want to shoot," said Ben. "Can we try that the next time we come?"

Fisherman scuffed his feet around. "I don't know. My uncle would be so mad. But I know where he keeps his outside guns."

Outside guns. Great.

Then Fisherman got that embarrassed look on his face again, the one he got when he talked about the old dog. "Hey, it's cool having you guys here," he said. The way he said it made me think he wasn't used to hanging out with friends.

Ben clapped him on the back. "Thanks, man," he said.

I said I was having fun too. And I was.

After that, we took the jumps apart and put everything away. While we worked, I kept an eye on the horse, who watched us the whole time. King trotted beside us when we rode our bikes down the road, and when he reached the end of the fence line, he snorted. I stopped to watch as he tossed his head a few times and then took off running, his black mane and tail flying.

I'm not sure how to say this, but hanging with the guys and riding bikes and petting a horse and being in a barn made everything else go away. I wish you could have been there.

Rodney

17

Hey, Larry,

A few more things from the longest day ever.

When my mom got home that afternoon, she was full of news and it was all bad.

"We'll pick up your sister when we go to see your dad on Saturday," she said, after checking to make sure I hadn't chopped off one of my arms from being left alone. I'd got changed so she couldn't see that I was dirty and covered in bruises and cuts and also had a major sunburn. If she noticed, I planned to tell her that I went into the backyard to study. Ha. As if. There aren't even any chairs back there. Just dirt and a few dead blades of grass.

I told her I was too busy to go, even though I a hundred percent wasn't. She just ignored me.

"And I got a call from the school today. They wanted to know where you were."

I was on the couch, staring at the game that I was now losing.

"I said you weren't feeling well, but that you'd be back tomorrow."

"No, I won't," I said.

"Rodney, if you don't go to school, you'll get referred to a truancy officer. The lady at your school told me all about it. If you miss another day without a doctor's note, you can be arrested and taken to detention."

I stared at her. Even though Ben and Fisherman told me about the rules, part of me thought they were exaggerating. They took kids to jail for missing school?

"That's right," she said. "That's how they do things here."

"You need to write me a note," I said. "Say I'm busy. I'm riding my bike in a Rockin' Energy Blitz commercial."

"A what?"

"It's an energy drink."

"You are not allowed to drink those. And you are not busy. Rodney, these people aren't fooling around about school attendance." It was the first time she'd said something that wasn't trying to put a positive spin on our new situation. That worried me. But not enough to make me go to school.

"Tell them I'm still sick. I *am* sick, technically. Sick of this town counts."

My mom's sigh was so big it practically made the curtains move.

"Rodney, you and your sister are understandably traumatized. But I don't think the reporters will be back. The reaction to those photos and the video was not good."

I felt my mouth fall open.

"What photos? What videos?"

"The ones of us. Especially you."

"Us? *Me?*"

"People felt it was exploitative. I don't think they'll target us again."

"There are pictures *and* videos?" I said again, like someone without ears.

"You don't need to look. They're in trash publications and on terrible websites. We didn't do anything wrong. All we can do is keep moving forward and live our lives."

I thought of what my sister would say if she was home. "We need to live our best lives," she'd say, mimicking my mom's attempts to be positive. My mom was deep into the best life theory and I used to agree with her. If you have a few lives to choose from, always pick the best and most fun one. It's what the Rules are all about. I've noticed that I keep forgetting the Rules. I don't want to get lucky anymore. I just want to get through this. I don't know how you feel, Lar, since I haven't heard from you. Sorry if that sounds harsh.

Anyway, then my mom said she was sorry, but she had to go teach an exercise class. I was surprised, since I had been alone, or at least said I was alone, all day. I didn't say anything though. I just told her to have fun.

She came over and kissed the top of my head.

"You are the best kid. I love you and things will be okay. It's just going to take time. There's a turkey pot pie in the oven. I set the timer. Please don't forget to take it out. Use the oven mitts."

As if I would forget. There are things that matter and pot pie is one of them. Not burning your hands is another one. Maybe that should be the eleventh rule: don't burn both hands.

Then I told her I might have a job.

She stopped dead.

"Who offered you a job?" she said. "You're eleven. You can't work."

"I'll be twelve soon," I said, even though my birthday is still five months away. "And it's not like that. One of the kids at school said he works on his uncle's ranch. I said I could help out there too."

"You want to work on a *ranch*?" she said, like I'd just said I wanted to get a job getting my fingernails pulled out by goblins.

Then she snuck a look at her watch, which was good because it's best to ask for things when she's got to be somewhere.

"I thought that if we're going to live here for a while, I should learn about how to do stuff like that," I said.

Her face softened. "That's really smart, Rodney. And responsible. We'll talk about it more, but it sounds promising."

"I need my own bike," I said. "So I can get there if they hire me."

She grabbed her gym bag from the kitchen table. "Good thing I've got a second job!" she said.

When I went online, I had a message from Rigmor.

130

Rigmor: Where were you today?

Me: Sick.

Rigmor: See you tomorrow?

I wanted to jump up and down. She wanted to see me!

But then I remembered that Rigmor wasn't the only person at school. There were all the stares and the whispers and Lallie the braidiac saying she didn't feel safe around me and Macii the whisperer researching my personal life.

Me: If I feel better. But I might still be sick.

Rigmor: Are you well enough to play V?

Me: Yes!

For the next hour, I played *Villainous* with her and I was Darth Vader and she was Bane and she beat me. Then I heard the timer go off for my pot pie, so I stopped playing while I ate. I was so busy playing and eating that when my dad called, I didn't answer either time.

Hope you are good.

Rodney

18

Hey, Larry,

Okay, you are not going to believe this!

Even though I wanted to see Rigmor and Ben and Fisherman and some of the other people, I stayed home from school today again and the truancy officer actually showed up at the house! After he told me who he was, I asked him to put his ID under the door so I could inspect it.

"It doesn't fit," he said. "But you can call the school to confirm who I am."

I was hiding from the school, so I didn't want to call them. It was easier just to let him in. So I opened the door.

"Rodney?" he said. He was standing on the front step and he completely blocked out the sun.

I almost couldn't answer because if he had lied and didn't really work for the school district and was here to abduct me, I wouldn't stand a chance. The guy looked like a major appliance. He could probably run right through the walls of this house, leaving behind the shape of a huge truancy officer carrying a stupid kid.

"How are you doing?" he asked.

I was staring at his arms. Each one was the same size as my body.

"I work out," he said.

"A lot," I said.

He laughed. "Yup. So, Rodney, I'm just checking on you."

Even though he was massive, his face wasn't mean.

"I'm sick?" I said.

"Are you?"

"Kind of." I felt embarrassed for lying. I actually felt quite good from being well-rested and having so many snacks. I liked skipping school, even though I was also pretty bored already and it was only the second day.

"The thing is that the school called your mom again and then I called her. She says you're not sick, you're just refusing to go."

I nodded. That was true.

"My sister's not going either," I said, like a tattling four-year-old.

He made a little face, and I could tell that argument wasn't convincing him I should stay home from school.

"Your mom told me that."

"My sister should really be at school," I said.

"The high school has their own truancy officer. You have to deal with me. You want to talk about it?"

I shook my head. I really didn't want to talk about it.

"My name is Timoci."

134

"You have an accent," I said, because I was nervous, and he did have an accent.

He smiled and looked even friendlier.

"I'm from Fiji."

"Where is that? Fiji, I mean."

Because I stopped going to school and was probably going to be a sixth-grade dropout, I forgot all my geography. I wonder how long until I forget math and English too.

"Same general part of the world as Australia," he said. "Well, it's actually pretty far from Australia."

"You don't sound Australian." I know because we had an Australian nanny for a while until she quit all of a sudden. Also, an Australian guy gave us skiing lessons once. Timoci's accent was different than theirs.

"That's 'cause I'm from Fiji."

Right then there was a noise behind Timoci. A throat-clearing noise.

We both turned.

Timoci turned around and I saw my mom standing at the bottom of the stairs. She looked all business-y in her suit. For some reason, it just dawned on me then that it was probably upsetting for her that she couldn't make me go to school just like it was upsetting for her that Kate didn't want to eat or go to school. Or stay here.

"Hello," said my mom. "I'm Victoria Creder—I mean, Garzi. Thank you for coming."

"Hello," said Timoci in his accent that sounded so relaxing, especially compared to my dad, whose voice is usually the opposite of relaxing.

"Hey, Mom," I said. Then I thought about her words: Thank you for coming? She *invited* him here?

I gave her a how-could-you look but she didn't notice.

"Rodney, Mr. Timoci is here to speak to you about going back to school."

"Just Timoci is fine," said Just Timoci.

My mom smiled.

Ugh.

"I know," I said. "He said."

"Let's all go inside and discuss," said my mom.

Timoci tried to step aside for her, but he was too big, so she backed down the stairs, and he went down the stairs and let her go up and then he followed her, and it was like watching the worst marching routine ever. I wished I had a jet pack so I could jet away to, like, Australia and go surfing in a place that had no sharks, and maybe after that I'd go to Fiji where I'd be safe from Timoci.

He sat on the chair and I was worried it was going to collapse. My mom sat beside me on the couch.

"So, Rodney, you're not wanting to go to school, eh?" said Timoci.

"Not really."

"Things not good there?"

I stared at him in a way that I almost never stare at people. A rude way. "Nothing's good here. Or there." Which wasn't true, but I said it anyway.

He looked at my mom.

"It's been a tough transition for all of us. I think I explained some aspects of our, uh, situation on the phone."

"Yes," he said. He sounded so nice and sorry for us that it made things worse. Even truancy officers felt bad for us.

"Can I go to my room?" I asked. "I'm not feeling well."

"No," said my mom. And for once she sounded tough. "You need to sit here and listen."

That was pretty shocking. My mom never plays hardball like that.

"Your future is at stake. You can't keep missing school. And I can't drag you there. I have to work."

"If you want, Rodney," said Timoci. "I can pick you up. Drop you off. No one will bother you."

Oh yeah, that would be good for my social life. Getting picked up and dropped off by the truancy officer.

"What about Kate?" I said. I really am sort of a rat fink.

"I'll deal with Kate," said my mom. "When we pick her up on the weekend."

"At least *I* didn't run away," I said.

"Rodney," said my mom. "I can't handle much more. Don't you even think about running away."

I looked down.

"If you won't go to school, I'm going to have to report you. If I have to do it two or more times, the judge will order you to juvenile hall. It's not a good thing. You don't want it," said Timoci.

I couldn't believe it. A judge! Juvenile hall?

"It's not going to go that far," he said, his voice still soft but really deep. I hoped I'd grow up to have a voice like Timoci, but I probably wouldn't. I'll just have a boring voice. "Like I said, I can pick you up. Drop you off? We can start today. I'll take you into the office to get a note."

I looked at my shoes and thought of the horse at Fisherman's uncle's ranch. Riding King would be even better than a jet pack. I could ride him into the desert. We'd go so far, no one would find us. If he could swim, maybe we could go to Fiji.

"So are you ready?" he asked.

I looked down. I was wearing pajamas.

"I'll get dressed." I went in my closet room, and after I left, I heard them laugh and her say something about Pilates. How nice for them.

So Lar, you now know someone who has basically been arrested by a truancy officer.

Rodney

19

Hey, Larry,

If you're wondering how the rest of the day was, all you need to see is the in-class assignment my social studies teacher gave us, which I've attached here.

Social Studies Assignment In-Class

Name: __Rodney__

Please discuss THREE of the following topics, using examples.

1. How does the media influence public perception of major events?
2. Are some media sources more trustworthy than others? Explain your answer.
3. How does ownership of media influence coverage?
4. What is propaganda and how does it work?
5. Define sensationalism in media.
6. Discuss social media uses and abuses.

1: I think the media gets it wrong all the time, even though they should know better. They don't know everything, even though they act like they do. And they don't care about people and write about stories that ruin people's lives. But the <u>New York Times</u> and the <u>Washington Post</u> are slightly better than some of the other ones because of how they research both sides and are not as biased.

2: The <u>Las Vegas Profiler</u> and the Scoundrels and Liars website are garbage because their reporters follow celebrities around and even their kids, which is unethical. Also, Fox News is propaganda because it just tells one side of the story.

6: Social media is terrible because people just try to get attention by making fun of other people and shaming people who might not have even done anything wrong. Also, selfies are boring and people should really get lives.

After we finished, the teacher read some of our answers out loud in front of everyone. At least she didn't read mine out loud. I think she just gave us that assignment to find out what I'd say.

During the lunch hour, I saw at least six people watching the Van Johnson video and then staring at me. I didn't go to the benches to see Dave in case Macii was there. Rigmor was at a track meet, so I didn't see her at all. Ben and Fisherman invited me to go to the Gas Pro Stop and Shop convenience store to get candy. I said no because I wanted to be alone.

In our last period, which was gym class, Lallie told the teacher that I was staring at her in a way that made her feel upset and "violenated," and the gym teacher told her the word was actually "violated." Then he didn't seem to know what to do because Macii spoke up and said she felt the same way about me. He said the girls should run laps outside on the track and the boys should run laps in the gym.

When the girls walked out of the gym, some of the boys watched them go and one whistled and said something rude about their shorts, and the teacher told him AND ME that if we kept it up, we'd be suspended. In my whole life I never whistled at someone or said anything rude about what a girl or anyone else was wearing! I would never do that. Okay, maybe I have whistled at one of those ice cream sandwiches made with homemade cookies. I love those things. But I would never do it to a person. It was awful. The whistling *and* being blamed.

"Nice job, jerks," said this guy who all the girls like and who hangs around with girls all the time.

"I never—" I said, but he was already running past me.

The guy who said the rude thing ran next to me. His name is Keven and he does stare at the girls. All the time. It even makes me uncomfortable.

"Everybody's too sensitive. Especially girls," he said. "Nothing wrong with looking."

I didn't nod because I didn't agree. No one likes to get stared at, plus I was having trouble breathing because I was having an anxiety attack from how bad the day was, and I don't think girls are too sensitive. I think *I* might be too sensitive. I definitely wouldn't want Keven staring at me.

When I didn't answer, he said, "Whatever," and ran off, because he's way faster than me.

So I ran alone, feeling like I was going to die for almost the whole time.

I extra hate school now.

Take care,

Rodney

20

Hey, Larry,

It's decided for sure now. I'm never going to send this to you. For one thing, it's really long, so you might not have time to read it, even though you read more than almost anyone I know. For another, your mom might not want you to hang around me now that I have a truancy officer. But I still like writing you, so I'm going to keep doing it, if you don't mind. Which you won't, because you don't know. Ha.

Anyway, we were in Vegas again on Saturday. Same deal as before. We got up super early. Even though Kate wasn't there, I got in the back seat and slept until we hit the city. When I looked at my mom in the driver's seat, she had her headphones on. She was probably listening to one of her inspirational talks. My dad used to make fun of how she likes stuff like that. I was glad she never let it stop her.

She seemed so content, driving along, that I didn't want to bother her. I just stayed still and thought my thoughts.

When we pulled into the treatment center, I sat up in my seat, pretending that I was just waking up.

"Oh, honey, you're awake. I hope you had a good sleep," she said.

"Yup." I fake yawned and real stretched.

She turned to look at me, headphones around her neck like a DJ. "This visit will be facilitated by a counselor. As we discussed last time."

I nodded and didn't sigh, because my sister says my sighs are passive aggressive, which is not true because I don't do anything aggressive, ever.

"They're going to let us in the back door in case of photographers."

"Will Elizabeth be our counselor?" I thought back to the calm gray lady. Talking to her might be okay, if I had to talk to someone.

"That's right."

"Will Cardi and Yates be there?"

"No. Thank god."

I was glad not to talk to Cardi, but I'd have liked to see Yates.

It was the same routine when we went inside as the last time, only Kate wasn't with us to make comments, which I half missed and half didn't miss, which is sort of the way I feel about Kate in general.

My mom asked the big receptionist guy, whose name turned out to be Derek, if Kate had arrived yet.

"Not yet," said Derek.

After he searched us, he took us to the meeting room. It was empty.

"We'll wait for Kate to arrive before we get started," he said.

Derek seemed like a good person. I wondered if he felt bad for my dad for being falsely accused and having to go to a treatment center to calm down about it. Or maybe he judged my dad for teaching people how to gamble. Even my dad says some people should leave it alone because they go overboard and they aren't good at it.

My mom and I sat at the big table and she started playing with her nails, which is something she only does when she's very nervous. She takes good care of her nails and doesn't like to do anything to damage them.

"She'll be here soon," she said, and the way she said it made me think maybe she didn't think Kate would show up.

"Yeah," I said.

I was just about to ask Mom if I could go to the bathroom when Derek came back. "Kate's here," he said.

"Thank goodness," said my mom.

"But she's not alone. She brought two friends. For support."

My mom's mouth fell open.

"She did what?"

"She says they're 'emotional support friends.' But they aren't on the visitor list. What would you like me to do?"

"Lavender and Cavendish?" asked my mom.

He nodded, and instead of looking all calm and stable, he looked like he just dealt with my sister.

"Let me speak to Kate," said my mom.

Here's something I bet you don't know, Lar. Lavender's and Cavendish's real names are Linwood and Trixie, so you can see why they'd want to change them. It's weird, since the new names aren't better at all. But Lav and Cav are loyal to Kate and so I like them for that. Loyalty is a good quality and one it seems like my old friends don't have. I'm not trying to be rude when I say that. Well, maybe I am, I guess. You probably have your reasons for not returning my texts or DMs. Not that I've sent any lately. I guess I just felt bad when I saw my sister still having her best friends.

When Derek and Mom brought Kate and Lav and Cav into the room, I was happy to see that Kate looked less pale and the dark circles under her eyes were lighter. She was still extremely skinny, but regular skinny, not scary skinny like she was before she ran away. All it took was a few days away from us and she looked better. Cavendish and Lavender eat a lot more than Kate, and they always talk about how not eating is what men want women to do so men can have all the power because women are so starved they can't stand up for their rights. Then they go on and on about the patriarchy, which is about men running the world. Remember how we used to think they were saying "the Petrarch," and we didn't know what a Petrarch was, so I looked it up and we found out that Petrarch was an Italian poet? I didn't understand why a poet who had been dead for hundreds of years would be interested in whether my sister eats or not. Then your mother explained it to us. You know, I think that was one of the last times I talked to your mom.

Cavendish actually wore her hair off her face but not in a normal way. She had her bangs in a ponytail on her forehead. She looked like a unicorn, only instead of having a horn, she had a fountain coming off her head. You'd have liked it, probably.

"Kate is not going to talk today," Cavendish said, and her forehead tail bounced. "She's still processing and wants to do so at her own pace."

My mom looked at her. My mom always looks so normal compared to Kate and her friends. She looks like she should be a billboard for tooth whitener, and they look like they are on a poster about extremely troubled teens in the counselor's office at school.

"Okay," said my mother. She's very patient with my sister and Lavender and Cavendish, even though they treat her like she's dumb, which she is not.

"Are you willing to speak to the counselor?" my mom asked Kate.

My sister stared at her and made a face without even seeming to move her facial muscles.

"You all need to speak to Kate through us," said Lavender, who had dyed her hair gray and curled it really tight so it looked like she was wearing an old lady wig.

"I'm sorry?" said my mom, still looking at Kate.

"Please speak through her intermediaries," said Cavendish. "That's us."

"We are her spokespeople," said Lavender. "She's been through enough."

Kate nodded.

They were being very strange, as usual, but it was sort of funny, and I was glad they were with us. It made me wish I had a friend there, but I'm not saying that to make you feel bad.

147

Then Elizabeth came in with her long, real gray hair hanging all the way to her waist, practically. There was a man beside her who was shaped like a rutabaga, which we both agree is the funniest vegetable.

Elizabeth was staring at Kate and Lavender and Cavendish, and I wondered if she was jealous that Lavender also had gray hair, even though she's only a teenager. Maybe it's something everyone really wants to have now.

But instead of glaring at them, Elizabeth smiled, like the sight of them made her feel better about everything.

"Hello," she said. "It's so nice to see you all."

Kate and her friends stared back at Elizabeth and a little bit of the mad went out of them. Even they couldn't be too angry at a soft gray cloud.

"Hello," said my mom.

"I'd like to speak with Rodney first," said Elizabeth the Cloud.

I sort of jumped because, to be honest, I sort of forgot that I was there and that people could see me, which I do sometimes, as you know.

I wondered who was going to have to talk to the rutabaga man. I hoped it was Kate via Lavender and Cavendish.

"Hi," he said, and he had a really deep voice, like a sportscaster or radio announcer or something. Then he told my mom she would be speaking to him before the family conference.

My mom nodded, and picked up her bags.

"And us?" said Cavendish. "Who are we and Kate seeing?"

"I'll be recording the whole thing with my phone," said Lavender. "For legal purposes."

"I'll be back to speak with Kate . . . and you, if that's what Kate wants, after I speak with Rodney," said Elizabeth.

Before I got to hear or see any more, Elizabeth opened the door for me, and we left the room, followed by my mom and her deep-voiced rutabaga counselor.

I'm going to stop here because I need a snack. Family visits, even ones with professionals in charge, are extremely tiring, even to remember.

Back soon!

Rodney

21

Hey, Lar,

I'm back! But you aren't! Ha, ha!

So here's what happened.

Elizabeth brought me into her office. It looked more like a plant store than an office. There were plants on the windowsills, on the shelves, on the floor, and quite a few hanging from the ceiling. Some were flowering and other ones were climbing up strings attached to tacks in the walls. They all looked very healthy. Her job must be very stressful for her to need so many plants.

We both know how hard plants can be to take care of, although you were better at it than me. Remember in third grade when we all got a little spider plant to look after? And we kept them on this special shelf, and if we wanted, we could bring our plant to sit on our desks during reading time. We had to water them and take off their dead leaves and give them plant food. I worked hard on my plant, but it turned yellow and died after a few months. Our teacher said I had loved it to death by overwatering it and putting too much compost on it. Later, I heard her tell the custodian that she'd never seen anyone kill a spider plant before. Everyone else's plants lived. Some of them even had baby spider plants. Is yours still all huge and healthy?

"Rodney?" said Elizabeth.

"Yes?" I tried to act like I had heard everything she said before I started thinking about my dead little spider plant, even though I hadn't.

"How have you been?" she said. "Since you were last here?"

It's hard to believe it had already been three weeks since our last visit.

"Good," I said, which was obviously a total lie.

"I'm glad." She smiled. I smiled back.

"I understand you haven't wanted to go to school. Because of the situation with your father."

I thought of Timoci from Fiji and how he was probably going to put me in detention prison.

"I'm fine," I said. "I'll go."

"Your parents tell me you don't like conflict," said Elizabeth. She wasn't being as relaxing as I hoped. Now I was sort of wishing I got the rutabaga guy instead of her.

I didn't answer.

"Have you spoken to anyone about what's going on in your family?"

I stared at her happy plants. Wished I was eating a pot pie. I didn't tell her I was writing to you because it seems like a weird thing to do, especially since you're never going to read this.

"I know you haven't spoken to either of your parents about what's happened. Have you spoken to any of your friends?"

"We moved," I said.

"That must have been hard. Your parents said you really liked your old school and you had good friends there. Are you keeping in touch with your friends from home?"

"No."

"Have you tried to contact them?"

I was NOT ENJOYING THIS CONVERSATION, so I decided to stop having it.

"I need to use the bathroom," I said.

Elizabeth sighed. "I'm sorry to pry, Rodney, but it's my job. If we're going to have a productive and honest family meeting, I need a sense of where everyone is at."

I wanted to say that where I was at was in a treatment center in a plant-y office getting asked too many questions. But I didn't.

She sighed and I felt bad for her. She was a nice lady. Excellent plants.

"Do you remember where the bathroom is?" she asked.

I nodded and went to find the bathroom. It was locked, so I kept going down a long hallway. The next one was busy too. I went down another hallway and saw a room full of kids and teenagers, sitting in chairs arranged in a circle.

One of them noticed me.

"Hey!" she said. "Get in here, you!"

I went in. Why not?

"I bet you're looking for us." The girl was a teenager, about my sister's age, round and kind of cheerful. She had

Lego-bright clothes and her blonde hair was curly and shiny. I liked her right away.

I didn't say I was looking for the bathroom. I didn't say anything.

"Gang! We got us a nontalker here. That means you sit in that part of the circle."

I went and sat in an empty chair between a kid who was probably around seven or eight and a girl around my age. They looked at me and didn't say anything. I appreciated that and decided I liked them too.

"Those of us who talk were just discussing how fun it is to come here every weekend to visit our people," said the blonde girl. "We're being extra sarcastic."

I nodded.

"I'm Lindsay, the teen facilitator of the Rebound Group. My mother has been here"—she pretended to look at her watch—"for about two hundred years and three months."

"I thought you said she'd been here twice before," said the tall kid next to her. He had new Jordans and wore a bright-blue sweat suit with white stripes down the arms and legs.

"That's right. Two stays one hundred years each. How do you think I got the title of teen facilitator? My family practically has shares in this joint."

"You exaggerate, Linds," said the boy in the sweat suit.

"It's how I cope. In all seriousness, new kid, my mom has been here three times. She enjoys pills and has bipolar disorder. We all like it when she's in here because at least she's safe. What's your person in for?"

"Linds," said the sweat suit guy again. "He's in the non-talking section. Get off his case."

The kid next to me nodded.

"I was trying to startle him into sharing," she said.

Then the four kids who liked to talk, talked about what they'd be doing if they weren't visiting family members. It turned out they wouldn't be doing much, except the kid in the sweat suit, who was here to visit his aunt, who was his mom's twin sister. He was a dancer and would be making a video with his crew when he finished visiting. He was the coolest person in the room by about six miles.

What I learned from listening to the kids was that the patients at the treatment center drink, take drugs, gamble, and some of them are addicted to gaming, or they have a mental illness. It's called the Chase Clinic because of the doctor who started it.

I didn't say anything, but I was confused. My dad didn't take drugs or drink that much. He gambles, but he's extremely good at it. He was accused of something he didn't do. Maybe that gave him emotional damage?

I wondered if my sister was going to end up in this group. She and Lavender and Cavendish would be the queens of it, along with the other talkers.

I'd been in there about five minutes when Elizabeth poked her head in.

"Ah, Rodney. There you are." She didn't look mad. In fact, she looked sort of happy. "You've found our Rebound Group."

"I got lost," I said.

"This is a good place to get lost to," she said.

"Hey, Elizabeth," said the talkers.

"It's good to see you all," she said. Then she turned back to me. "Rodney? Are you ready to come back to my office?"

I nodded, got up, and waved at the kids in the circle.

"Later, Rodney," said the sweat suit kid, whose name was Zach.

"Come back and see us so you can not talk some more," said Lindsay.

When Elizabeth and I were back in her office, she closed the door.

"That group has been useful for many of our patients' family members."

My mind was busy with questions. Why *was* my dad here instead of in a lawyer's office getting his name cleared? I admit, there was also the part of me that didn't want to know what he was doing in the Chase Clinic.

I stared at a plant that had leaves with triangular edges, like the spine on a dinosaur. There were bright-pink flowers at the ends of the spiky leaves. I wondered how long it would take me to kill it.

"Rodney," said Elizabeth. "I understand that you don't want to talk, but ignoring this situation and shutting down won't make it go away."

I looked at her. "I know."

"None of this is your fault, but unfortunately, you have to live with the aftermath and it's going to influence your life."

My ears started to buzz, I think from how much they didn't want to hear.

"You have more control than you think," she said. "And part of that control is knowing how to respond to the facts."

"I think I'd just like to listen," I said. I heard a kid in the group therapy say that when Lindsay asked him to share. I liked the way it sounded.

"Oh, Rodney," said Elizabeth. Then she sighed, but in a way that wasn't mad. It was more patient and understanding. "There's nothing you'd like to say before we begin the family meeting? Nothing you'd like to say about how this situation has affected you? Questions about what happened and what the future might bring? This is an opportunity for all of you to speak up."

When I spoke, I said something I didn't expect. I'm not telling you to make you feel bad. It's just what happened. "I don't understand why my friends aren't getting back to me." I said friends, but I meant you. After the first few days, I stopped texting Trelawny and Emily and Monty. All we really had in common was the name ending in *y* thing, now that I think about it.

"That must hurt," said Elizabeth.

"I guess."

She waited for me to say more.

"I've messaged my friend Larry a bunch of times. He never gets back to me. No one does."

"I'm sorry," said Elizabeth.

"Maybe he's busy," I said, because I didn't want to be mad at you, even though I was really, really mad at everyone. And you.

"Maybe it will just take time."

"For what?" I asked.

"For your friends to process. They might not know how to handle this."

What did that mean? What was "*this*"? I was the one whose dad was in treatment for something he didn't even do, and I was the one who had to move away.

"I wish Larry would come here. Like Kate's friends did. We've been friends since we were in preschool."

Elizabeth looked at me and her gray eyes looked sort of sad, which made me wish I'd never said anything. I hate making people look sad.

Elizabeth leaned toward me. She smelled like a field with flowers in it.

"Rodney, I want you to know that you can handle this. No matter what's happening in your family or in your school, or with your friends, you can handle it. The feelings that come up might not feel good, but they are important. They are real."

"Okay," I said. I hoped Missy Stephenson and anyone else who accused my dad wasn't feeling good either. They were going to feel especially terrible when my family sued them and got all their money.

"I need to speak to your sister, briefly," she said. "And then it's time for our meeting."

We'd been at Chase Clinic for less than an hour and it felt like the longest year of my life.

I probably don't need to tell you I'm taking a break due to how I'm feeling about everything. I'm blue, man. Blue all the way through.

Whatever.

Rodney

22

Hey, Larry Who Will Never
Read This and Who I Am Mad At,

Here's what happened in the rest of the visit. Not that anyone cares.

My dad looked just the same as he did the last time. Hard to believe it was only three weeks ago. It felt like a year but also like we never left. Maybe a bit hairier. His sort-of-beard was longer, and he had on his favorite button-up sweater and his old Star Wars T-shirt. He says he has no plans to grow out of his style. My sister used to try to steal the shirt, but he always stole it back. That was back when things were good.

He was at the head of the table. My mom and I sat on his left and my sister sat on his right. Cavendish and Lavender sat against the wall, I guess because they aren't family.

I tried to sit beside them, but Elizabeth said I needed to sit at the table.

"Rodney," said my dad. "Hey, my guy. I've missed you."

"Thanks, Dad," I said. "Me too."

"Welcome, everyone," said the rutabaga in his announcer voice. "Our goal here today is to open the channels of communication. Let's start by talking about how we're doing."

Kate stared at him in her meanest way. "We?" she said, even though she wasn't supposed to be talking.

"It's a figure of speech," said Elizabeth. "But we're glad to hear your voice."

Kate went quiet again.

"This is about you guys. We're just here as facilitators," said the rutabaga.

"There are more facilitators than family, if you count us," said Cavendish. Lavender nodded.

"We're going to have to ask you girls not to interrupt," said the rutabaga.

"Fine!" said Cavendish. She mimed turning a key in front of her face.

Rutabaga looked at my mom. "Would you like to start?"

My mom took a deep breath. She didn't look at my dad when she talked.

"I feel angry and hurt and confused. And ashamed, Jeremy. I feel very ashamed."

My shoulders got all tense. Even my knees started to hurt.

"You have nothing to feel—" said my dad, but rutabaga stopped him.

"Let her finish, please."

"I know *I* have nothing to be ashamed of. But there it is," said my mom. "Our lives have been turned upside down. The damage you've done to us is incalculable. And those other women, women I *know*. Women I care about. I feel like I should have known. Like there's something I could have done. Which means that I also feel guilty."

"I—" said my dad, but the counselor held up his hand. For a root vegetable, he was pretty commanding.

"Now, I get to sit with these feelings. We all do. And I get to pick up the pieces while you hide out here," she said.

All I could think was that she didn't know Missy Stephenson. Who was she talking about? And I guess I also started to wonder what he did. Why did she have to be ashamed my dad hugged people too much?

My dad didn't try to defend himself. He just stared at the table.

This was definitely getting my vote for one of the least fun family activities ever.

"Kate?" said Elizabeth. "Do you feel like saying anything?"

I was glad Elizabeth didn't use the word "share." My sister hates the word "share" and the people who use it.

Kate glared at my dad. Her crooked bangs were growing out, so only her right eye was visible. It was angry enough for both eyes.

"I'm trying not to hate you," she said. And then she started crying. She got up and went to sit between Cavendish and Lavender, who moved to let her in. They put their arms around her.

I thought I was going to throw up. It was hard to breathe. I wondered if I might be dying. I used to have such a fun life.

"Rodney?" said Elizabeth. "Is there anything you'd like to say to your father?"

I shook my head.

"MAKE HIM TALK!" shouted Kate. "It's not fair that he gets to just tune this out while the rest of us are having the worst time of our lives. I bet he doesn't even know half of it."

"Come on, Kate," said my dad. "Get off his case."

"YOU DON'T GET TO TALK!" yelled Kate.

"I'll pass," I said, only semi-violating my no-talking policy. And then, because I don't have very much self-control, I kept talking.

"Why aren't we suing them? Or at least Missy Stephenson?"

Everyone looked at me. My dad didn't seem to know what I was talking about.

"The women. The ones who lied about you. Are we going to sue them?"

My dad swallowed like he had something in his throat and was afraid he was going to choke.

"I want to sue Van Johnson. And those reporters who came to the school."

"I . . ." said my dad. "We . . ."

"Rodney," said my mom. "Why would we sue the women?"

Everyone was very still.

"Because they're lying. Right, Dad?"

"Some things have been misconstrued," said my dad.

And then everyone started talking at once.

"Jeremy, you need to come clean," said my mom.

162

"Why don't you tell him what happened?" said Kate.

"I think we need to dial it down a bit. Give people time to collect themselves before we continue," said Elizabeth. But no one listened to her. Especially not me.

"Dad, why don't you explain about Larry's mom?" yelled Kate.

I felt like someone threw a bucket of ice on me. And lit me on fire. And stabbed me a bunch of times.

I got up. Larry's mom. *Your* mom.

"Rodney," said my dad.

"Rodney?" said my mom.

"Rodney!" said everyone.

I didn't answer. I just got up and left.

I don't know what to say, man. So I won't say anything.

Rodney

23

Hey, No One,

I didn't say a word on the way home. Not even Kate spoke, which was fine with me.

But when we got to our dumb, stupid new house in our dumb, stupid new town where everything is bad, something surprising happened. After she put away all the snacks we didn't eat, which was a lot, my mom went into her room. When she came out, she was pushing a bike for me.

It was a BMX. The frame was painted copper and it smelled like metal and oil and rubber.

"I noticed your friend rides this kind of bike. It will be easier for you to do things with your friends if you have one too."

"Thanks, Mom," I said. And then I felt sort of surprised because something good happened and that made me start to cry a little bit.

"Oh, baby," she said, and she hugged me, which was hard because the bike was between us. But she got it done, because my mom is awesome.

"Make sure you wear a helmet," said Kate, who was sitting at the kitchen table watching us at the same time as she was FaceTiming with Lavender and Cavendish. "You have exactly no brain cells to spare if you have a crash."

She might be right.

I asked if I could go for a ride. It wasn't going to be dinnertime for an hour or so. Mom said to hold up for a second. She went back in her room and came out with a new silver-and-black full-face helmet, which is not what BMXers wear, when they wear helmets at all. But I still liked it.

I rode down the street as fast as I could. In some places the air was still warm from the sun, and it was cool where shade was spreading off the mountain. I rode so fast I couldn't think about anything.

Rodney, Man of No Words and No Thoughts. Man of no friends.

I rode past the front of the school where the reporters got us and I flipped it the bird.

I rode my new bike around the back of the school and onto the field that Fisherman had run across carrying me so he could smash me into the soccer net. I probably wasn't supposed to ride my bike on the grass, but I didn't care. I just rode in circles. A couple of times I even put up my middle finger but that didn't feel right, so I put it back down. I did some not-very-good bunny hops and tried an endo and nearly tipped over onto my face. There was a good chance I was turning into a bad kid. Good thing I already have a juvenile delinquency officer.

Finally, I got tired of wrecking the field, so I rode my new bike to the Stop and Shop. I had never been to a convenience store by myself before. There weren't any near our old house because it was sort of a fancy neighborhood and you had to drive a long way to buy anything. But all the kids around here go to the Stop and Shop and apparently a lot of them steal stuff. I knew because of all the signs. I went in with my mom when we first moved here, and there was a sign on the front that said no groups were allowed in and kids had to leave their backpacks at the front and be accompanied by an adult and criminals would be prosecuted and another sign saying Your Stealing Costs Everybody. Me and my mom joked about how the signage wasn't very welcoming.

My mom didn't give me a lock with my bike, so even though there was no one around, I pushed it into the store.

"NO BIKES!" yelled the guy behind the counter. He had a handlebar moustache and was dressed like a cowboy. Not a real one, but more like a Halloween cowboy. Me and my dad would have had the best laugh about him.

I was going to explain that I didn't want my new bike to get stolen, but then Ben pulled up outside on his bike. He was in front of pump number one, like he was going to put some gas in his bike.

I left the store and wheeled my bike over. He whistled. "Nice," he said.

"My mom got it for me."

"You need me to watch it while you go in?" he asked.

"Yeah. The guy won't let me bring it inside. You want anything?"

He nodded. "Purple Slusher." Then he held my bike by the handlebars with one hand and rode around with it like he was leading a pony while I went into the store.

After I got us each a Slusher, which would have made my mom give me a big lecture about the effect of food dyes on my immune system, I saw the clerk waving out the window to get Ben's attention.

"Move, kid! Cars need to get in there," he said, even though there weren't any cars around.

By the time I got up to the counter, the guy was so mad that he'd gone outside to yell at Ben. While he did that, I stole two chocolate bars. I didn't even look at what kind they were. I just kept an eye on the camera on the wall while I put our drinks on the counter. When I reached into my pocket with one hand to get my money, I grabbed the two bars with the other hand so the camera couldn't see. It was the most dangerous thing I ever did, except jumping into the gorge and being unsupervised at a ranch.

When handlebar guy came back, he stared at me hard, like he suspected me of stealing something. And I stared right back from inside my helmet, but my knees felt kind of wobbly. He couldn't see my face properly and neither could the camera. It's extremely easy to turn into a delinquent.

Outside, I gave Ben his drink and we got on our bikes and rode off. He didn't put his hands on his handlebars. I tried to copy him but I nearly wiped out and I spilled half of my drink all over my hand and nearly fell over a bunch of times, but I pretended having sticky, freezing ice water all over my hand didn't bother me. We rode all the way back to the school, where we went down some railings using his pegs and gapped the stairs and hit a few walls.

Then we started messing around in the dugout. Ben found a tennis ball and we threw it against the wall for a while and then we sat on the bench, just sort of being. It was relaxing.

"We went to visit my dad," I said.

"How was it?" asked Ben.

"Lame."

"Yeah," he said. "I talked to my mom this morning."

"How was that?" I asked.

"Kind of hard. She cried. She always cries."

"Sorry," I said. "My mom cries a lot too."

Ben threw the ball up into the air and caught it. Over and over.

"If I go see her, I might not be able to come back," he said.

"That's rough." I thought about saying more about my dad and the visit, but I thought it was better to listen. And I didn't tell him he should go visit his mom because then I would lose my only real friend here. That was self-ish, I guess.

Ben stopped throwing the ball and just held it on his chest as he stared at the roof of the dugout. Someone had written a bunch of swear words up there. We both noticed it at the same time.

"Must be hard to write curse words up high like that," he said.

"Do you think they brought a ladder?"

"That was no tiptoes job," he said. "Maybe they put a felt pen on, like, a long stick or something."

I gave him one of the chocolate bars I stole. They were both Butterfingers.

"I stole these," I said.

"Why?" asked Ben.

"I don't know. Same reason the person wrote that on the ceiling, I guess."

Ben sat up. "I know I like to push things. It's kind of a family thing. You know, with the sports and stuff. But there are things you shouldn't push, man," he said. "It's just not worth it. My dad and my mom tell me and my brothers to keep our noses clean. Even a guy like you needs to be careful. When things go wrong, they can go real wrong."

I didn't completely know what he was talking about. After all, he did illegal jumps off cliffs and rode around school fields on his bike and broke bones.

"What do you mean, a guy like me?"

He smiled. Ben was pretty handsome, like his brothers. Maybe if you are extremely fit, you get good-looking. I'm just average, but maybe I'll get more exceptional if I keep riding the bike.

"A white kid," said Ben. "A rich one."

"We're not rich," I said.

"Yeah, but you still seem sort of rich. Your mom drives those fancy wheels. You dress like a golfer or something. If you are only rich some of the time, it stays on you. Even when you're not rich."

I thought about that. Maybe he was right. If you started out poor, did that stay on you?

"I don't like to give advice or anything, but if you have problems with your dad or whatever," he said, "you don't have to let it mess you up. You can be your own man."

I wanted to tell him I was proud of my dad, but I didn't. Because I don't know what kind of man my dad is anymore. I thought about what Kate said about Larry's mom. I'd been trying not to think about it. I didn't want to know what my dad did to her, or to Missy Stephenson. Or why the female interns on his show quit all the time. Why Van Johnson wrote a song about him. I guess I'm the kind of guy who doesn't want to know stuff. And being a man was feeling terrible in general.

Interesting note: the fact that chocolate bars are stolen doesn't make them taste any better or worse.

Rodney

24

Dear Void,

Okay. That makes no sense. Dear Journal? Dear Universe?
I don't know. Maybe it doesn't matter. Maybe I don't care.

On Sunday, Ben was already waiting outside our house
before I finished eating breakfast.

"That kid with the bike is out there," said Kate, who
actually ate yogurt with a few quinoa puffs sprinkled on
top. Like about seven. It was a start.

"It's Rodney's friend," said my mom. "Want to ask him
in for breakfast?" she asked me.

"No. We're going for a ride," I said. Ben didn't seem
like the kind of friend who would want to come in to meet
my mom or sister. He was too wild.

"Okay, honey. Be safe and have fun."

Before I could get out the door, she asked about pro-
tective gear. "I noticed that some of the kids wear knee
and elbow pads. Should I get that for you? I'm getting
paid soon."

The grateful and excited way she said it made me feel sort of sad.

"It's okay. We're just bombing around."

"I know some kids like to do tricks and things on their bikes. I want you to be safe."

"We will. And I'm not good enough to do tricks yet."

"Oh good," she said. "That's a relief." And then she laughed.

Ben and I rode over to meet Fisherman, who was waiting for us by the school.

"Hope you guys brought a lunch this time," said Fisherman. "We can't go into my aunt's kitchen again. She'll tell my dad and then I'll get it."

"Your aunt and uncle at home?" asked Ben.

"They're at an auction. Farm equipment."

The morning was like every morning in Stony Butte. Bright and cool. The sky was crossed with pink and orange streaks. If I had no brain filled with memories and wonderings and worries, I'd have been bright green. When my brain forgot to think, the way it did when I was riding a bike, or stealing, or petting King, or talking to Ben or Rigmor, I even felt sort of happy. That was a surprise. How things can be terrible but then they can change to be not-terrible just by thinking about something else or doing something else.

We didn't talk while we pedaled. They were on mountain bikes and I was on my BMX, so I was even slower than usual. Finally, Ben told me to hang onto his seat and he towed me. Fisherman had a bottle of water stuck in a cage on the frame of his bike, and Ben wore a little backpack

174

with a hose running from it that he drank from. I totally forgot to bring water. Not a smart thing to do in the desert. I guess I was still getting used to being the kind of person who goes outside without an adult and does adventures.

The first thing I looked for when I hit the fence line at Rancho Socorro was King, but he wasn't there. The ranch looked a little softer in the morning light, but that was the only difference. Same truck with the flat tire. Same shiny orange tractor.

The old dog lay in front of the barn and he wagged his tail in the dirt when he finally noticed us, which took a while because he'd been sleeping.

We leaned our bikes up against the barn and then all went to say hello to Willy the dog, who didn't get up.

"He's stiff in the morning," said Fisherman, like he didn't want anyone to criticize the dog.

"Sure," said Ben. "Everybody is."

I was pretty sure Ben wasn't.

"Think we could do some target practice?" asked Ben.

Fisherman put his hands in his pockets. "I don't know," he said. "I'm not supposed to touch guns when my uncle's not here."

I nodded. "Yeah," I said. "That's probably a good rule."

"We could each do a couple of shots. Like at a target," said Ben. "I never shot before. My dad's too Canadian to let us have a gun. But I bet I have good aim."

"Man, I been shooting since I was six. You ain't going to beat me," said Fisherman.

I wanted to tell them how dangerous it was for anyone to use guns, but especially kids. We learned all the

175

statistics in school. But maybe it would be like when I said we used to have an Olympic-length pool.

Using a gun sounded like the worst idea ever, but before I could talk them out of it, I saw King galloping across the scrubby field toward us. He looked like a horse in a commercial, his head high, his tail flowing, kind of like we had important news and he couldn't wait to hear it.

"Here he comes!" I said, and my heart went faster the closer he got. He was so cool it made me feel a little choked up.

"You going to shoot?" asked Ben.

"No thanks. I'm going to see him." I was staring at the shiny horse who was craning his head over the fence at me. He was the coolest thing ever.

I didn't bring water, but I did bring six carrots from home that I stuck in the waistband of my shorts. We don't have any sugar cubes because my mom and sister think sugar is from the devil.

When I got to King, he sniffed my hair and my face, and I admit I kind of sniffed him back. I never knew how the smell of a horse could make a person feel calmer and more alive.

"Hey, boy," I said and held up a carrot. He lipped it out of my hand.

I was so focused on the horse that when a shot sounded behind me, I nearly jumped out of my shoes. King's head went up and he shifted his feet, but he didn't run away.

My plan was to just pet King until Ben and Fisherman finished shooting. I didn't want to be anywhere near that.

I fed him the next carrot and listened to him crunch and tried to ignore the gunshots. King must be used to the noise because it didn't seem to bother him.

Maybe I could quit school and work at a ranch. Maybe I could work at *this* ranch and never go home again and never go visit my dad again. Fisherman's uncle could teach me how to look after the ranch and how to ride King, and I'd be this famous ranch guy, or maybe not even famous. Maybe just a guy who rode around on a nice horse. And maybe Rigmor would want to ride double with me on King.

I felt my face get hot at the thought.

There were no more carrots, and Ben and Fisherman had stopped shooting, so the air seemed extra still and quiet. I was glad they were done. The shooting stressed me out.

I wanted to get a little closer to King, so I climbed through the fence. I was halfway in, one leg inside and the other outside, when I felt him take a little nibble of my hair. That made me laugh and feel sort of proud, somehow.

Once I was inside the fence, I didn't know what else to do, so I petted his neck and touched his mane. I wanted to feed him something else, so I walked over to a big tin tub. The grass just outside the fence was long and bright green from where water must have spilled. It was just out of his reach. He followed me like a dog while I reached through and picked him grass. He took it from my hand just as nice as he took the carrots. I bet he'd had his eye on that green grass for a long time.

What I really wanted to do was hug him around his neck, which is weird, but somehow I had this idea that if I

177

could do that, everything would be okay, even though we were living in Stony Butte and my dad was hiding out in a treatment center and everyone thought I was a creeper and my mom was sad and my sister was mad and I was afraid all the time.

I stood there, and King dropped his head a little and sniffed my hair. Then I put my arm around his neck and he let me. He smelled like goodness and dirt and grass. If there's such a thing as horses, the world can't be all bad, I thought.

That's when the next shot came, and it sounded way closer than the others. Something darted by, close to the ground, going so fast I couldn't even tell what it was. It went right behind King.

King jumped so high he was like a kangaroo instead of a horse. He knocked me down with his chest, and all at once I remembered how big he was, how wild. Then he went up on his back legs, front legs pawing, right over top of me and then like in a bad dream, he fell over backward. His body made a heavy thud that shook the ground.

At first I was afraid to get off the ground. But he didn't move, so I started kind of crawling toward him. He lay a few feet away, on his side, his legs out straight, like a dead cartoon horse.

"King?" I said. He didn't move.

"Are you . . . ?" I asked in a whisper.

I realized with a sickening feeling in my stomach that one of the bullets must have hit him. Ben or Fisherman must have tried to shoot some animal and accidentally shot King instead. They shot him.

I knew we shouldn't have played with guns. A scream started in my throat, but it got stuck there, burning a hole in my chest until it blasted me straight up.

It took me a second to hear Fisherman yelling at me.

"What did you do to him?" He was yelling while he scrambled through the fence.

"What?" I said. "Nothing."

"You can't go in there," he yelled. "I told you to stay out of the pasture."

He ran over and dropped to his knees.

Ben spoke from behind the fence. "Oh man," he said. I looked back to see him standing there, long gun hanging at his side.

"Come on, buddy," said Fisherman, putting a hand out toward King's head, like he was scared to touch him. "Get up or my uncle's going to kill me," he said.

I couldn't breathe but I was also about to cry, which meant I was probably going to die because you need to be able to breathe to cry. I walked to the fence, slipped out, and Ben stood back and watched me, and he didn't say anything and neither did I. Maybe he was the one who shot King. Or maybe I killed King by putting him in the line of fire.

Why did I come here? Why was no place safe?

I ran to my bike. It lay with the other ones in the dirt at the side of the driveway. I dragged it upright, and when the pedal got tangled up with the spokes on one of the other bikes, I started to yank on it and yank on it.

"Rodney," said someone. I'm not sure who. But I still wasn't really breathing and thought that I was going to pass out if I didn't get away.

I finally got my bike loose and I jumped on and started to pedal. I was wobbling all over the place and nearly fell, but I didn't, and soon I was pedaling so hard I couldn't even keep up with myself. It was like my feet were spinning on nothing. My thoughts spun too—pictures in my mind of King laying there, dead, and my dad not answering when I asked when he was going to sue the ladies and Lallie saying I made her uncomfortable and Kate asking my dad to explain about Larry's mom. My whole stupid body was crying now. It was like being punched all over.

I didn't look back. Just rode and rode and rode and felt the invisible punches land.

25

Dear Diary?

About an hour after I got home there was a knock at the door. I thought it might be the police, come to arrest me for being involved in gun theft and the shooting of an innocent horse. The thought made me almost start crying again, even though I was so dehydrated it was hard to believe that I had more tears. I drank four huge glasses of water as soon as I got home, and I kept having to go pee every ten minutes.

One thing TV and movies taught me was that you had to answer the door when it was the police.

My mom was at the community center teaching Pilates classes for the afternoon, and Kate was locked in her room. I was glad no one was around. All the crying would have upset my mom and showed how much less tough I am than my sister.

Ben was on the front step.

"Hey, Rodney," he said. He had his bike helmet on. He really wears that thing everywhere.

"Hi," I said. And I gulped. Told myself not to lose it again.

"The horse is okay," he said.

All at once I felt about twenty times better. And that made my eyes start leaking again. I rubbed a fist into them to try and make them stop. I think I might have a problem. What kind of person cries this much? What kind of guy?

"Yeah, he was just dazed. I guess he's done that before. Fallen over and sort of knocked himself out." Ben made a gesture with his hand to show the horse falling over backward. "Boom," he said.

"That's good," I said, trying to control my breathing and not show my emotions.

"Fisherman's aunt came back early, and he is *in trouble*. Like massive trouble. It's good you left when you did."

"What kind of massive trouble?" I asked.

"Like she threatened to tell his dad, who would—" Ben punched a fist into his hand twice to show what would happen to Fisherman.

I felt my mouth drop open and my eyes dry up. "His dad will hit him?" I said. My dad would definitely never do that.

"Yeah. I think he's a hard man. But then Fisherman's aunt said if he makes amends, she won't tell anyone. She said he's going to be working on that ranch for free until he's twenty-five."

I thought about Fisherman's dad hitting him. My stomach was upset from thinking about it.

"She muttered something about telling on me, but I don't think she'll do it." I noticed he put his finger on the doorframe, like he was touching wood. "Guess we shouldn't have played with those guns," said Ben. "But they should probably keep them in a safe or something. It's pretty dangerous, when you think about it. Kids could get at them."

I didn't tell him that technically we are kids. And I didn't go near them. All I did was go in a pasture to hug a horse. And steal some chocolate bars.

"I just wanted to tell you it's okay. The horse is fine. And Rodney?"

I leaned in. "Yes?"

"My friend, you have got to relax."

Then he turned, jumped down the stairs, ran along beside his bike and then jumped on and was gone.

My friend.

Then I got a text from Rigmor. She asked if I wanted to meet her at the track. She said she didn't want to run laps alone. I hoped that meant I could just watch her, because I was tired. But I said yes, even though there was a risk of running.

My life has a lot of serious problems, but at least I have stuff to do and people to do it with.

Rodney

26

Hey, Universe,

Me again. I'm not done yet! This is like the never-ending story!

Anyway, when I got to the track, Rigmor was stretching. I felt sort of strange and empty after all the stuff that had happened.

"You going to run?" asked Rigmor.

I had on shorts and a button-up shirt. And my helmet.

"I don't think so," I said. "I'm kind of tired."

"You going to take off your helmet?"

I took it off and put it on the grass.

Rigmor straightened up and looked at me.

"What's wrong?" she asked. It was strange how she seemed to know me even though we just started being friends.

Her nearly white hair reminded me of people in Holland. We went there once when I was eight. I remember people being really tall. And they put chocolate sprinkles on white bread. I wish people did that here.

"Is Norway like Holland?" I asked her.

"Not to Norwegians," she said. "And anyways, I was born here."

"Your hair reminds me of Holland," I said. And then I felt dumb. And maybe creepy. "Sorry," I said.

"That's fine."

Then all at once it came out and it was all jumbled up and messy.

"I don't think my dad is like your brother."

She stopped moving.

"I'm worried he did what those ladies said he did."

Rigmor looked serious. "Why?"

I shrugged. "I don't know. He's not trying to defend himself. He's kind of hiding in that center. And other stuff. It makes me wonder. But I don't want to know. He's my dad."

Rigmor sighed. "I'm sorry," she said. "That would be terrible."

"I wanted to tell you. In case you don't want to be . . . to hang out."

"You're not your dad," she said. She sounded just like Ben. It seemed so obvious, but I guess I always thought my dad was the best part of me.

Rigmor looked around the field. I wondered if she felt uncomfortable being alone there with me.

"Ready?" she said.

"Sorry?"

"Ready to run?"

"I'm still kind of—" I flopped over on my side to show how tired I was.

"You're fine. And I need someone to pass so I feel like I'm winning." She laughed. It was a nice laugh.

So I ran around the track way slower than her and we slapped hands when she passed me, which she did about ten times. I'd never done anything like that before. It was fun, even though my legs were noodles after two laps. But they weren't as bad as they would have been when we first moved here. I'm getting pretty active, I guess.

When she was finished, she stretched, and I lay in the grass and stared at the sky. They have nice skies in Stony Butte.

Then I walked with her to meet her brother, who was waiting in the parking lot to take her home.

She leaned into the driver's side window, where Nils was playing on his phone.

"Nils," she said. "Rodney's got something to say."

I looked at her. Why did she keep doing this to me?

Nils looked up. He has her blue eyes.

"What's up?" he asked. Not smiling.

I stayed silent, standing just behind Rigmor.

"Tell him," she said.

I wondered if all Norwegians were so direct.

"I, uh," I said.

"He thinks his dad did what they say. Rodney's worried about it."

Nils nodded, slowly. "That's too bad, man. Your dad's so talented. And he always seemed cool."

Which was almost exactly how I felt.

"Nils is sort of friends now with the girl who accused him," said Rigmor.

"Who?"

"The girl who said he touched her. Nils talks to her now."

"Yeah, she always says she's sorry," said Nils.

"What do you say to her?" I asked.

"Nothing. I say it's okay." He made a little huffing noise.

"What do you want to say?" asked Rigmor.

"I want to say that if you like someone, that's fine. But if they don't like you back, it's over. Show some respect." He sounded irritable.

"Nils is dating one of that girl's friends now. Awkward!" said Rigmor.

"You're twelve. What do you know about awkward?" said Nils.

"I know some things," said Rigmor.

Her brother laughed and his face lost that hard look it had sometimes. "That's true."

Rigmor punched me lightly in the arm.

"Later," she said. "Thanks for running with me."

I nodded.

She got into the car and Nils turned it around. He stopped the car beside me, his arm hanging out the window.

"You need to talk to your dad," he said. "Directly."

Then they drove away.

So that's what I decided to do.

More later. This is hard.

Rodney

27

Hey, Team of Counselors I'm Probably Going to Need After All This,

I walked in the front door and found my mom and sister sitting at the table.

"Can we go to Vegas?" I asked.

They both stared.

"Now?" said my mom.

"I want to talk to Larry."

My mom's eyes went wide, and Kate put her hand to her mouth.

"Oh, honey," said my mom. "I'm not sure that's a good idea. It's three o'clock now. And it's a long drive."

"I want to talk to Larry, and then I want to go see Dad."

My mom puffed out a breath.

"Maybe we could just go see your father? How about I make an appointment?"

"I need to talk to Larry now," I said. I wasn't sure why, but I knew it felt important.

"We better do it while he's willing," said Kate. And I thought she was probably right.

"Let me call Larry's mother," said my mom. There was this worried look on her face like calling Isbell was the last thing she wanted to do.

"But, Mom—" started Kate.

"Hush," said my mother. "Let me figure this out."

Five minutes later we were in the Range Rover, heading for Vegas.

My mom couldn't get through to Larry's mom. She just got a message that the number could not be reached.

"I hope your dad's treatment center lets us in. We won't be there until late," muttered my mom.

I didn't care. If they wouldn't let us in, I'd wait on the doorstep until the next morning. You know how once you decide to do something you've been avoiding, you need to do it right away? That's how I felt then.

The drive seemed to take forty hours instead of four, and it also seemed to take no time at all. When we hit the city, it was still light out. We drove into our old neighborhood. Everything looked the same but way fancier than I remembered. I used to think that most people had nice houses and at least a small pool and went to private school and had nannies and all that. Now I know most people don't. Now we don't. When we lived here, our parents and teachers were always telling us how lucky we were and how we should be grateful. They were right and they weren't. Our new life isn't bad, thanks to my mom getting me a bike, and Rigmor and my new semi-dangerous friends who are cool in their own way.

It's weird to think Larry will never read this. Probably no one will. But if someone else does, I want you to know that Larry would understand about my new life. He was always more responsible than the rest of us. His parents are divorced, and his dad lives in Europe half the time for his job, and his mom has, or at least had, a busy job, but they also do charity stuff and help poor people. We never did that. My parents probably should have made me do more charity things so I would be as mature as Larry.

"What's the plan?" asked Kate, when we were about five minutes from Larry's.

I shrugged.

"I don't know if this is a good idea," said my mom. Her face was sort of shiny because she went straight from teaching her class to driving all the way to the city. Or maybe she was just nervous. I know I was.

"Are you sure you're ready for this?" said Kate, turning around to look at me in the back seat. "I don't think I could do it."

"Are you sure you don't want to go see your father first?" said Mom. "Or at least talk some things through before you talk to Larry?"

"No," I said.

We pulled up the steep driveway to Larry's place. The light was soft and a little yellow, the way it gets in Vegas later in the day. Larry's house is a little smaller than our old house.

It's tall and made of wood and metal and has big windows. Out back there were cool winding stone pathways we used to use to do sword fights. They have a kidney-shaped

191

pool with a fountain. You can't do laps or play water polo in Larry's pool, but it's still fun to cool off in there when it's hot. Larry usually came to our house, because my mom was home more than his and our pool was huge. Plus, we had a games room and his mom had to work a lot. Just like my dad. Thinking about his mom and my dad turned my stomach.

"I'll come with you," said my mom.

"Isbell's car's not here," I said.

Isbell doesn't park in the garage because she has a pottery studio that she never uses in there.

"Maybe Larry's not here either," said Kate. She sounded like she hoped he wasn't.

I got out of the car. When I was halfway to the door, I looked back to see my sister and mom watching me through the windshield, like they were afraid I was going to fall into a sinkhole.

I pushed the bell. My chest felt a little tight.

Footsteps inside.

"Yes?" said a voice through the security intercom. Isbell. Her voice is deep and kind of raspy. It's the kind of voice that is used to giving orders.

"Is Larry home?"

"Rodney?" she said. "What are you doing here?" She never asked me that before. She always seemed happy to see me.

"I would like to talk to Larry."

She sighed into the intercom system. It sounded like the wind at the beach. Then she unlocked and opened the door and we stared at each other.

Isbell looked the same as always in her T-shirt and jeans and feet in sandals, her hair in a wild Afro. My sister always said Isbell had the best style in Vegas. Then she would say that Larry had the worst style in Vegas because she gets uncomfortable being too nice about people.

"Rodney, I don't know if this is a good idea," said Isbell. Then she looked past me at the Range Rover.

"Is your mom here?"

I nodded. "And my sister."

"You're all here?"

"Not my dad," I said, and she made this face. It gave me a sharp pain in my side or my head or maybe all over.

"Can I talk to Larry?"

Isbell bit her lip. I wondered why she wasn't at work, but then I remembered that she worked on my dad's show and there was no show anymore. And it was Sunday night and nothing made sense anymore.

"Mom?" Larry appeared behind his mother. He looked at me like he was happy to see me, but then his face changed, and he looked like a totally different person.

"Rodney has come to see you," said Isbell, still with her hand on the door. She hadn't invited me in and she'd gone pale.

"Oh," said Larry. His glasses were slightly crooked and his shirt was buttoned wrong, but he still looked like my best and oldest friend and seeing him made me miss him more. Larry was a big part of what made my old life nice, and Larry was one of the nicest people I knew. *Is* one of the nicest people.

"Is it okay?" he asked his mom. "For me to talk to him?"

193

Isbell's face went funny, like she was going to cry, and I wished everybody would stop crying, including myself.

"I'm sorry, Rodney, there are a lot of things going on. I'm not sure this is the best time for you to be here. I'm sorry, boys."

"My mom's in the car," I said. Even though she already knew that. "Maybe you guys could talk."

She frowned at me. "I don't want to speak with your mother, Rodney."

It hurt my feelings to hear that.

"Why?" I said.

Her mouth fell open. "Rodney, have your parents spoken to you about the, uh, situation? With your father?"

I shook my head. But before I could explain that they tried, at least my mom did, she got really mad.

"Unbelievable," she said. "Are you telling me that your parents sent you over here on their behalf without explaining things to you? Are you freaking kidding me?"

"I thou—" I said, but she was storming past me and over to the Range Rover. I looked at Larry and he looked at me and then we watched our moms.

Isbell got to the car in about two seconds and knocked on the driver's side window.

"I can't believe you. You want *me* to tell him what your husband did? What he's been doing? How is this *my* responsibility? Just like I had to clean up after all the messes and avoid his . . . advances myself? So I could keep my job in order to support my son?"

"I—" said my mom.

"You're not much into dealing with reality, are you? How dare you put this on me. And these kids. You need to take Rodney to see his father so his father can explain himself."

Isbell was holding tight to the sides of the driver's window, talking at my mom like she wanted to scream at her but was trying not to. "I wish I didn't blame you, but I do," she said.

My heart was smashing around in my chest from how mean Isbell was being to my mom. This was my fault. I just wanted to talk to Larry.

I was still frozen in the doorway when Isbell stormed past me into her house.

"These kids deserve better," she said, yelling at my mom. "And so do I."

Then she shooed me out of the way and slammed the door.

I got into the car. My mom pulled out. When we were backing out of the driveway, I looked at Larry's window. He was there and he waved. I waved back.

No one said anything for a while until my sister spoke up.

"So that went great," she said.

My mom looked at Kate and then at me in the rear-view mirror. "Isbell is right," she said. "She's absolutely right. We need to speak to your father. All of us."

I have to take a break. If I ever write another story, I hope it's about something easier than this.

Rodney

28

Hey, Larry,

Who am I kidding? Obviously I'm writing to you, even if you never will read it. I guess I don't blame you if you don't. I wouldn't want to read what I've written here either. But thanks for texting after that thing at your house. I know you're not allowed to talk to me because of your mom suing my dad. But I was happy to hear from you. Don't be sorry about your mom. None of this is her fault.

What happened after we left your house is that we went to my dad's treatment center. When we all got out, my legs felt funny. My mom knocked on the big wooden door. It didn't make much of a sound. I was jealous of that door. How solid it was. How no one would be breaking it down or opening it unless it wanted to be opened.

It was starting to get dark, and I was that kind of tired you get when you feel sort of sick and also like you are never going to sleep again as long as you live.

"Ring the bell," said Kate. Then she got impatient and reached over and rang a little buzzer I hadn't noticed before.

Silence and then someone opened the door. It was the front desk guy. Derek. He must work about twenty-four hours a day. He didn't look surprised when he saw us. He seemed like the kind of guy who was never surprised about anything. I'd like to be like him. A combination of him and the front door.

"We're here to see my husband," said my mom.

Derek watched us, like he was deciding what to do. When I grow up, I'd like to have smooth skin like Derek, but I'm probably going to have skin like my dad. My dad's one of those guys who looks like he has to shave all the time. Right now, I'm not sure I want to have anything in common with my dad, including facial hair.

"I'll have to get a counselor to sign off on this," he said. "This is well outside regular visiting hours."

My mom leaned in, and the way she did it, you could see for a second how strong she is. In her core. If I keep riding a bike and doing dangerous outdoor things, I might get as strong as my mom.

"The time is now," she said. "My son is ready to talk, and my husband has a job to do. This is not just about him."

Derek nodded. "Good for you," he said. "Come in."

This time, there were no people in the living room area. I wondered where all the patients were.

"Pretty dead around here when it's not visiting hours," said Kate. "Poor Dad. He hates peace and quiet. He likes things busy."

"I'm sure he prefers this to the situation he's going to find himself in when he gets out," said my mom. "Sorry, kids. That came out harsher than I intended."

Kate held up her hands. "No need. I like it! Sparky! More of that please."

My mom gave Kate a stare like the one she gave Derek. A strong core stare.

"For reals, Mom. You sound like you're done taking the old merde-oh."

"No swearing, Kate," said my mom.

"It's French. Doesn't count."

We sat down in leather chairs. Listening to my mom and my sister bicker at each other took my mind off my own thoughts. I didn't like it, exactly, due to not enjoying conflict, but it was better than being afraid of the future and thinking lousy thoughts. Maybe that's why they did it—arguing, I mean. Maybe it took their minds off everything.

Derek was behind the front desk, speaking quietly into the phone.

I tried to hear what he was saying but couldn't.

Then I stared at the carpet. It was very hotel-like. I've always liked hotel carpets because they usually have such interesting patterns. The fancier the hotel, the wilder the carpet. That made me think about Ben and Fisherman. Had they ever stayed in a fancy hotel with a complicated carpet? I had a hard time picturing it. I had a hard time picturing me in one too. My fancy hotel carpet days were probably over.

I actually jumped when Derek came over and asked us to come with him, because I was so busy thinking about carpets.

My mom grabbed her big bag and handed it to Derek; Kate gave him her lumpy pouch purse that she sewed herself when she and Cavendish and Lavender were trying to be "makers," because they can never just do stuff without giving it a trendy name.

"You have anything, Rodney?"

I shook my head and felt sort of sorry for myself that I didn't even have a wallet or anything. Maybe next year I'll get a wallet. Find some stuff to put in it.

Everything felt slowed down. Maybe if we all slowed down enough, we wouldn't have to go through with this.

Derek took us to the usual meeting room. It was empty.

We sat at the table. My mom kept looking over at me. I could tell Kate wanted to say something, but she didn't.

"Well, isn't this a lovely surprise," said my dad from the doorway. Derek stood right behind him.

My dad didn't look good. He was pale and his stomach looked bigger. He looked older than he used to. His whiskers weren't the cool kind, but more like the too-tired-to-shave kind.

I felt sort of sick looking at him because now he *looked* like he should be in a treatment center. I wished I was somewhere else. This was a mistake.

I could tell my mom didn't like the look of him either.

That made me feel even worse.

"Rodney would like to speak to you," said my mom. "He's ready."

"Look, darling, I don't know if this is a good time. I was in the middle of someth—"

200

"Your TV show can wait," said Derek. He squeezed my dad's shoulder.

"He's ready and that's what matters," said my mom when it looked like my dad was going to turn around and leave.

My dad sagged a little more. "It might be useful to have a counsel—"

"You can handle this, Jeremy. Kate and I will wait outside."

Then she got up and so did Kate. My mom walked past my dad without looking at him, but Kate gave his shoulder a pat. That also made me sort of sad.

"Jeremy, let me know if you need anything. And the counselor will be ready to speak to you afterward," said Derek from the doorway.

My dad sighed again. "That won't be necessary. But thank you. I can take it from here."

I felt almost dizzy. This was worse than when I jumped off the cliff with Ben. Worse than when Ben and Fisherman started shooting with the gun. But it *wasn't* worse than seeing King lying there and thinking he'd been shot. It also wasn't worse than having the reporters come to my school.

"Well, chum," said my dad, and I stared at him due to Chum being Fisherman's nickname. I almost forgot that when my dad's uncomfortable he calls people chum because he's English.

"I don't like being called that," I said.

His mouth dropped open. His lips looked dry. He wasn't used to me telling him what I liked and didn't like. None of us did that with my dad. I never noticed that before.

He rubbed a hand over his scruffy cheeks. "I'm sorry, Rodney. Of course not. How are things? Your mother holding up all right? Kate?"

I didn't say anything.

He cleared his throat. I waited.

"I gather the time is ripe for some, uh, explanations."

His eyes were bloodshot. He yawned, which was really strange.

"Sorry," he said. "I was watching television when Derek came to get me."

I didn't say anything. My dad never used to sit around. He went to bed late and got up early. He was busy doing lots of things all the time. Even at our birthday parties he would take calls and step out for meetings.

He yawned again. Like this was boring for him.

"Sorry, buddy. I'm just . . . I think it's a stress reaction. I've been sleeping a lot, lately. My counselor says I'm trying to hide from my feelings."

His feelings? What about my feelings? Mom's? Kate's? What about Isbell's feelings? Missy Stephenson's feelings?

Our talk hadn't even started, but I hated it so much I felt like I was going to throw up if it went on much longer.

"Rodney," he said, interrupting my thoughts. "What do you know about what's happened?"

My eyes felt like there was sand in them. "I don't know," I said.

"Don't try to be funny," he said. Like I would ever make a joke about this, the worst moment of my life, except for the moment when I thought King was dead.

"I know you were trying to date some women. On set and stuff. Like women who wanted you to leave them alone."

He wasn't yawning now.

He sucked in a deep breath and straightened his shoulders. His eyes were wet. So were mine and he hadn't even started talking.

"I have exercised bad judgment. Upon occasion. In work situations and elsewhere."

I didn't say anything because even I knew that wasn't an explanation.

"I have a problem, Rodney," said my dad. "And it has affected other people."

The hole in my chest felt like it belonged in space. Cold, black, and infinities-wide and deep. "What kind of problem?"

"I have been," he said. "Been—" His eyelids fluttered, like he was about to pass out.

What was he even talking about?

"What?" I said.

"I have been inappropriate. With women," he said. "With a number of women. Who were not your mother. I made them uncomfortable. I took liberties."

"Liberties?" I said. Liberties means freedom. He took the freedom of some women who were not my mother.

"I had feelings for some women who worked for me or that I met at work. And I behaved in a way I ought not to have done." His accent was getting stronger. "My behavior was inexcusable."

"What did you do to Isbell?" I asked. The words just fell out of my mouth.

His mouth dropped open and his face turned red and then a chalky gray.

"What I did was not in the least acceptable and I'm sorry. I'm so sorry. I really am sick at what my actions have done to your mother, who is the finest woman I know. And what I've done to you kids. I don't have a better explanation. I got carried away. With my feelings. I've always had a lot of feelings."

My eyes were more than just wet now. My nose was running and I wiped at it with the back of my hand.

My dad handed me a tissue from the box on the table.

"I made Isbell and some interns feel unsafe and uncomfortable. I did damage to their careers with my comments. With my behavior. I crossed the line with a guest. I betrayed your trust and theirs. I could not be more sorry, and in the future I will do better. If I get a chance."

"Did you hurt Isbell?" I said. My whole body felt like it was on fire and being pricked with needles, and I didn't completely know what I meant by hurt but I also didn't want to know.

Van Johnson's song rang in my ears.

Creeperman. My dad was a creeperman.

"No, of course not. Well, not . . . I didn't physically hurt her. I made suggestions. I said things in fun. Some of it was a joke."

Some of it. I thought about the boys at school saying things about the girls in their shorts and I felt sick.

My dad stared at his knees. "I thought I deserved to express myself. Express my feelings. I wasn't thinking. Some of my, uh, physical affection was not welcome. I should not have touched anyone without asking first."

Touched. My dad had touched people. I couldn't look at him.

"Isbell is Larry's mom, Dad."

"And she was my employee. I know I made a terrible mistake. Mistakes. That's why I'm here, trying to get to the bottom of it. Find out what makes me—what made me—behave in such a way. I think it must be something that happened in my childhood. My parents' relationship—"

"How many ladies?" I asked.

"What?"

"How many ladies did you do this to?"

"Rodney, these days females of the species prefer to be called women," he said and then stopped. My dad used to be one of those guys who told other guys not to be sexist. His words got hung up in my brain like plastic bags stuck in trees.

"How many?" I asked.

"I behaved in a misguided way with a, uh, number of women," he said. "Some of them didn't discoura . . . No. That's not true. I shouldn't have done it, no matter that some of the women clearly found me attractive."

I felt something tear. Dads shouldn't say stuff like this to their kids.

"It was not a huge number, but it was too many. I'm sick. And I'm sorry. For everything."

"Are you going to go to jail?"

My dad stopped moving. "I don't think so. My punishment is more likely to be of the financial variety," he said. "Punitive damages. And, of course, the incalculable damage to my reputation, not to mention my brand."

His brand? His reputation? What about our reputation?

Then we stopped talking. I thought of all the times my dad was so funny and made me and my friends laugh. How it was like a celebrity had stopped by our house when he was home. How everyone wanted to be around him, especially when his show was popular. How he swam with me and Kate sometimes, and took us to Holland and England and brought us along to meet celebrities. I was so proud of my dad. He was amazing. He was never mean to us or to my mom.

I used to have a good life and I used to have a cool dad.

Now I had this. My eyes weren't wet anymore. I was dried up like an old sandwich.

"We'll get through this," said my dad. "I'm going to make everything right. I'm just glad it wasn't worse. Nothing was done that can't be undone."

Tell that to Isbell and Missy Stephenson and the other ladies. Tell that to Larry and me and Kate and my mom.

I stopped listening. I just wanted to go home. To Stony Butte.

"I have to go, Dad," I said. The word "dad" sounded strange in my ears. Like a dead word.

He stood up. He smelled sour. He never smelled like that before. He came around the table and hugged me. I patted his back and felt bad for him. I felt bad for me too, even though I was a dried-up sandwich now.

So that's it, I guess. Can't think of much more to say.

Take care. And I'm sorry, man. I really am.

Rodney

29

Hey, Lar,

I'm nearly done with this. I promise.

After I left the room, my sister went in to talk to him, and after she was done, my mom went in. No one stayed too long. He came out and hugged all of us before we left, and I wondered if my mom and sister noticed that he didn't smell so hot and sort of hoped they didn't.

It was hard to imagine him and my mom together because she was in 3-D full color and he was a faded poster someone left on a lamppost for too long. I kind of knew then that they wouldn't ever be together again.

I have never felt as bad for anyone as I did for him when we left him there. We got to go home to our little house, with each other. That was better than living in a place with swirly carpets where no one told you that you were turning sour from the inside out.

When we got to the car, my sister broke the ice. "If you're too tired, I can drive," she told my mom.

"Very funny," said my mom. "So hilarious I forgot to laugh." But then we all laughed a lot, and when we stopped, I felt even worse for my dad, because I didn't think he was laughing back in the Chase Clinic.

It was totally dark out now and we were all hungry, so Mom took us to a Veggie-Go-Go drive-through, which is her idea of fast food, and we all got wraps and high-energy smoothies.

"This'll clean out the old bank account," said my mom. That should have made me feel embarrassed because no one in my family ever used to mention how much food cost before, but somehow it was okay, because she was spending the last of her money getting us healthy comfort food and that was really nice of her.

It was at a rest stop off the highway. There was desert all around us and the last clouds in the sky seemed to glow against the dark.

I saw Mom noticing that Kate ate her whole wrap and her green drink, but she didn't say anything, which was probably smart. Kate's not into doing the right thing, and if she does it, you should not make a big deal of it in case she stops.

"Ready?" Mom asked, when she got back in the car after taking our biodegradable wrappers and cups to the recycling bin.

I nodded. Even though I ate a lot, I still felt sort of empty.

"Do you guys have any questions? For me, I mean."

"I do," said Kate. "When are you going to divorce him?"

"Oh, Kate," said my mom. "We're not there yet."

My sister put her hand on my mom's arm. If I hadn't been buckled into my seat in the back of the car, I probably would have fallen down from shock.

My mom looked from Kate to me. "I wish I'd known what your father was doing, how he was acting. I guess I should have known. But I didn't."

"You didn't know?" I asked her.

She studied the steering wheel. Finally, she shook her head. "No one said anything to me. Not Isbell. None of the crew on the show. I was busy with you guys. And he was at work all the time." She turned to us. "I thought he was happy. When we met, he said he wasn't happy in his marriage. I thought I made him happy. He was a good dad. And a good husband, when he was home. No matter what else he did, he was those things. And they count."

Kate made a rude noise. "Good husbands don't go around harassing women. Good dads don't act like disgusting pigs, and they don't ruin their families."

My mom looked at her steadily. "No, they don't. But that's not all there is to your father."

"I really miss him," I said. "How he was."

My mom reached back for me. "Me too. And I know you both miss our old life."

"Not me," said Kate. "I like keeping it real with the no money and the no prospects. And I love having a power shamer for a dad. I think this whole thing is character building. What doesn't kill you makes you a better Instagram poet."

"Kids," said my mom. "I wish things were different, but they're not. The best thing you will ever learn is to

209

deal with what is versus what you wish was. This isn't our fault. But we have to cope with it. We live in Stony Butte for the time being and we are building a life there." My mom's yoga training means she likes to keep things positive. Normally, I tune her out when she gets too yoga-ish, but on this night I was listening. Wide open.

"What about Dad?" I said.

"I honestly don't know. He has a lot of consequences to deal with. But he will always be your father." She thought for a second, like she was trying to remember all the things you should say to your kids when your husband turns out to have been someone who you wish you'd never met. "And none of this is your fault."

"Oh, thank god," said Kate. "Or I might develop an eating disorder."

My mom jerked her head to my sister. "That's not funny, Kate. I'm deeply worried about your relationship with food."

Kate held up her hands. "Sorry. Dark humor is sort of my brand. Lavender and Cavendish keep telling me that not eating might make me feel like I'm back in control, but all I'm doing is giving up my power by becoming literally smaller. I don't want to do that, so I've decided to take up power lifting."

I laughed out loud at the thought of my sister with her short flippy hair and chest-high old-man pants and skinny wrists power lifting anything. Who needs power lifting when you're as funny as she is? My dad gave her that at least. And anyone could see that even though she was just sitting in a parked car with me and my mom, she was awesome. All that anger and meanness was going to be useful when she figured out what to do with it.

And I hoped she was going to eat more.

"And you, Rodney?" asked Kate. "You okay back there?"

"Larry's not allowed to talk to me because Isbell is suing Dad."

"I'm sorry, baby," said my mom. "You guys were good friends."

And then, because there was really nothing left to say, she started the car back up. On the drive home, I thought about my dad, the power shamer, and felt bad for him and for all of us. I also thought about how I felt more bad things and good things in the last twenty-four hours than I'd ever felt. It's very tiring, feeling things, but it's not uninteresting.

I wonder if you feel the same.

Love you, man.

Rodney

30

Hey, Lar,

One more for the road. And thanks for the message last night. I'm glad your mom says we can talk as long as we don't discuss the case. I can't believe Mr. Gomez and Mr. Magellan are getting married! It must be so weird for Mr. Magellan to be marrying the principal of the school. And congratulations on being made the captain of the Circle Square Ping-Pong team. You deserve it.

I'm going to write you once more because it's sort of a habit now. After this, I guess we can just text or message or whatever.

The morning after I saw you in Vegas and had the meeting with my dad, Ben showed up early. It was a professional development day for teachers and so we had the day off. No juvenile hall for me! He came up to the door and actually knocked. He'd never done that before.

My mom answered before I could get there.

"Hello," she said. "You must be here for Rodney."

213

Ben nodded but didn't speak. I don't think he's comfortable around parents.

"Hi," I said, standing up from the table, where we were about to have breakfast.

"I, uh," he said, and he tilted his head like he wanted me to come outside.

"You're just in time for breakfast," said my mom. She looked around Ben. "Oh, hello. Come on in!" she called.

A minute later Fisherman and Ben were inside.

"Nice to meet you," said my mom, holding out her hand.

"Mom, this is Fisherman. And that's Ben," I said, finally going over to meet them.

"Ma'am," said Ben, when she shook his hand.

"Hello, Mrs., uh," said Fisherman. "Mrs. Ma'am." Then his face turned bright red.

She pretended not to notice. "Come, boys. Have a seat at the table."

I almost forgot what it was like to have my friends in the house. Around my parents. Parent. Since we moved here, I always felt like I was running away from home, especially when I was with these guys. And they acted like no one would ever want them inside.

"We were about to have overnight oatmeal," said my mom. "But you know what? With Rodney's friends here, let's go all out. I'll make waffles."

My sister stared at my mom, her eyes bugging behind her fashion glasses that do nothing to help her eyesight, but are very ugly, which she likes.

"I'll toast frozen waffles," corrected my mom. "I don't actually know how to make waffles from scratch."

Fisherman and Ben looked from my mom to my sister, like they didn't know what to do.

My mom was in the old fridge, digging out a box of waffles. "They're spelt and buckwheat. Is that okay?"

Fisherman and Ben nodded.

She took a second look at Fisherman and took another box of waffles out of the freezer compartment.

"Kate, could you please put out two more settings?"

My sister, who was in a pair of brown cords that she probably stole from a home for retired English professors and a blouse with puffy sleeves the color of a pool-table top, rolled her eyes. "Sure thing, Martha Stewart," she said.

Then she stopped and stared at me. I could tell she was about to say something about the patriarchy, which is how she usually gets out of chores. But she just made a face and took down another two plates and cutlery.

We ate two boxes of waffles, and even Ben and Fisherman had some overnight oatmeal, which is oatmeal that my mom leaves overnight in milk and then usually doesn't eat because it has so many carbs. She put some dried fruit in it so it tasted less like uncooked oatmeal left out all night.

My mom asked Ben questions. He told her about his mom in Canada and how they weren't sure how they were going to work things out.

"That must be hard," said my mom. "Your mom must miss you a lot."

"Yeah. She thinks she might get a job as a body double for a movie that's shooting in Vancouver. But anyway, she's there and we're here."

"I'm so sorry, Ben," said my mom. "I hope you get to see her soon. But I know Rodney would miss you if you left."

"Mom," I said. But it was true. I will hate it when Ben leaves.

My sister found out that Fisherman's dad is on long-term disability after he got hurt at work, and his mom is a secretary at the biggest church in town. Fisherman has a box turtle named Yoda and a cat named Pauly.

"You want to be a biologist?" asked my sister, I guess because of the turtle and cat.

Fisherman smiled and looked like a completely different person. I realized I'd almost never seen him look anything other than worried or mad before. "It would be cool to study biology," he said. "But there's no money for school. We lost our old place a few years ago. Getting set up again took the college money." His face went back to looking worried.

"I'm sorry," said my sister. "Don't give up, okay?"

"Thanks," said Fisherman.

And I thought: who are these people? It felt like my mom and sister were every bit as cool as my dad, just in a different way.

When we left breakfast, my mom told us to have fun and be safe, and even though things were the same as before, and my dad was still a power shamer and we had no money, somehow everything felt better, maybe from all the carbs and all the talking.

We rode our bikes to Ben's and he loaned me a mountain bike. I didn't want to have to tell my mom I can't ride a BMX long distances. I also didn't want her to feel bad that she can't afford to get me a second bike. After we picked up the mountain bike we headed onto the trails that lead to the base of the butte.

Before we got very far, Ben had to fix a flat tire. Fisherman and I sat on a log while he worked.

"You see your old man?" asked Ben, who was bent over his bike.

"Yeah."

"How'd it go?"

"Okay, I guess."

Neither of them said anything.

"He screwed up," I said. "He did stupid things with some . . . people. Some women."

"Maybe they're doing false accusations," said Fisherman. "That happens sometimes."

I stared at my dirty runners and thought about Isbell and my sister and my mom.

"He did it," I said.

"That sucks, man," said Fisherman.

"My mom always says that a good man is respectful," said Ben, looking up from his bike. Then he looked quickly at me. "I'm not saying that your dad . . ."

I nodded. "Your mom and my sister are right. My dad has issues. My sister says he's a power shamer."

They laughed. "Your sister's funny," said Fisherman. "But, man, does she dress bad."

"Yeah. You should see her friends."

"You got to make your own way," said Ben. "You got to trust yourself."

217

"I think my dad's planning to apologize for what he did. But they're suing him."

"At least if he apologizes, he'll feel better," said Ben.

"One of the ladies was my best friend's mom."

"Yikes," said Ben.

"That's bad," agreed Fisherman. "But it's not your fault. Hey, you interested in getting a turtle? Yoda's pretty interesting. But he's real low-key. I can get you a deal. He always makes me feel better."

"Maybe," I said.

"And you could come to our church sometime. Our pastor helps a lot of people," said Fisherman.

"Maybe," I said.

Ben had popped the wheel back on his bike and was ready to go.

"I got good energy. Never had healthy waffles or cold oatmeal before," he said. "I feel like I could fly right now."

"I never had smelt before either," said Fisherman, pushing himself to his feet.

"Spelt," I said. "It's a grain."

"City people," said Fisherman.

We followed Ben along the single track until we got to a ravine. Someone built a narrow bridge over it out of slats that looked like something from Lord of the Rings. It looked sort of like a ladder you would never want to climb, never mind ride your bike on. The drop between the ladder and the bottom of the ravine was at least twenty feet.

"Ready?" said Ben.

Fisherman and I looked at each other.

If I was scared, Fisherman must have been terrified. He weighed at least twice as much as me.

"No," I said. "I'm not ready for that. Can we go around?"

Ben smiled. "Let me check," he said and rode out over the rickety bridge, cocky as if he was on a paved road.

"That guy is fearless," said Fisherman.

"I'll be back," said Ben, riding along the other side. "Let me just find a place for you guys to cross!"

Fisherman and I waited.

"Box turtles make good pets," said Fisherman. "Just don't let one hibernate somewhere where you can't find them. We lost Yoda that way once."

"You can come with me when I go to the store," I said. "I'll save up."

We stood in the forest of skinny, dusty trees at the base of the butte.

"Maybe after this we could go to your uncle's ranch?" I said. "I wouldn't mind seeing how King is."

"My aunt wants me to help unload some hay. For my punishment. You can help."

Then Ben appeared behind us.

"Okay, follow me," he said.

And we followed him to a trail that had a proper bridge, with railings and everything, and we came out safe on the other side.

Acknowledgments

I would like to thank the following people: my wonderful editor, Lynne Missen, as well as Peter Phillips, Shana Hayes, Sarah Howden, Lisa Jager, Tara Walker, Samantha Devotta, Shanleigh Klassen, and everyone at Penguin Random House; my agent Hilary McMahon, as well as Susin Nielsen, Andrew Gray, Jennifer Herbison, Brigitte Mah, Nafiza Azad, Lynn More, Hartley Lin, Délani Valin, and Robin Stevenson. Extra special thanks to Bill Juby, Aaron Banta, Scott Banta, Trevor Juby, and James Waring, who show every day what it is to be good men. Eternal gratitude to my mother, Wendy Banta, for all kinds of support, and deepest respect to all the people helping to make much-needed change in the world.